POND LIFE

Tales of the Wondrous
and the Macabre

Sam Kates

SMITHCRAFT
P R E S S

Printed in the United States of America. First edition, December 2012.
Smithcraft Press edition, March 2014.

"Celesta" was originally published in *Cambrensis*, September 2002.
"The Barton Method" was originally published in *Scribble*, September 2003.
"Room Eight" was originally published in *Dark Tales*, January 2004.
"When I Was Young" was originally published in *Scribble*, February 2003.
"Mere Survival" was originally published in *Scribble*, February 2004.

ISBN 978-1-62927-010-4

Smithcraft Press
1921 Michels Drive NE
Palm Bay, FL 32905

www.SmithcraftPress.com

Contents

Celesta

I see them from the corner of my eyes. They know that I'm watching.

They're not there all the time. They know when I'm anxious. Then they appear, giggling, snide, insinuating. They tell me things.

I try to catch them out, snap my head to one side. But they skip away into the shadows, giggling gleefully, like mischievous children. Shadows and shade are their domain, their playground. They're quick.

But they don't fool me.

I loved her from afar. The purest form of love, unsullied by thoughtless word or mistimed touch. I'd stand at the end of the aisle, pretending to examine the chutneys, and watch her.

Hair of spun gold, eyes of deepest blue, lips soft and red: she was a living cliché. A glorious cliché.

She had been chiselled from the finest clay, her nose, chin and cheekbones formed exquisitely, with loving care. And her hands! Such delicate instruments: skin translucent, a suggestion of an intricate blue network beneath, fingers long and tapered. Pianist's fingers. Or harpist's.

Occasionally, a strand of that golden hair would come loose from the band that restrained it and fall over her brow. She'd raise one hand

and flick it back, not knowing the effect this simple action would have upon me. My heart rate would speed up, my breathing become ragged and my palms would glisten with sweat. I'd have to put down the jar I was holding for fear of dropping it.

I always expected them to appear at such moments, but they never did. Not there. Too brightly lit, I guess.

Sometimes, she was tired. She'd raise both hands to cover her face, yawn deeply into them, draw them tightly down her skin and finish with a flourish by shaking her head. I suppose you can imagine the turmoil this caused me. Once I trembled so badly an old lady asked me if I was all right.

Who can explain why such simple, unthinking gestures should provoke such a passionate response? Who can explain love?

Dr Hassam says they're not real. A product of my imagination, he says.

Dr Hassam has a head like a coconut. It has as much dark wispy hair on the bottom and sides as it does on top. He wears thick black glasses with lenses that magnify his eyes, and he blinks a lot, owlishly. He sucks peppermints to try and disguise the smell of tobacco on his breath.

He doesn't fool me.

"You've been smoking," I say.

He nods his head gravely, but his face remains impassive.

"I can't fool you," he says.

"They're real," I say.

He shakes his head, slowly. His expression does not flicker.

"No," he says. "They're not."

I gave her a name. There could be but one.

You have the face of an angel, I thought. You have the hair of an angel, I thought. You have the hands of an angel. You are my Celesta.

Celesta! Ah, what sweet joy you gave me. I whispered your name as I watched you. I engraved your name on my soul. I fell asleep with your name on my lips. How I adored you!

I loved her from afar.

It was not enough.

Dr Hassam asks me questions. About my parents, my childhood, my dreams.

Then he listens.

I talk. Sometimes for hours.

I run out of things to say. I run out of memories. That's when I make things up.

Dr Hassam adjusts the pads attached to my temples. And he listens.

I like Dr Hassam. I want to please him.

I had to get nearer to her. Look into those eyes. See those dainty hands doing their work. Examine each strand of that golden hair. I might have the chance to breathe in her scent. Perhaps even talk to her. Oh, sweet, sweet Celesta!

I normally use a basket. I don't eat much. The express checkout is six tills away from hers.

That day, I used a trolley.

I had no idea what I was putting into the trolley. Tins of cat food, for all I knew. I don't like cats.

Then I was approaching her till.

She was serving somebody, hands in motion as she picked up items from the black rubber conveyor belt and passed them over the barcode reader. She infused even this mundane action with a heavenly grace.

I brought the trolley to a standstill. I had never been that close to her before. I stood and feasted my eyes upon her. What a sumptuous spread!

From that unaccustomed range, I noticed new things. Her finely-sculpted nose bore a light sprinkling of freckles. Her eyelashes were darker than her hair, auburn nearly, and curled outwards like Caribbean waves. Her ears grew tight to her head, two pink shells peeping from beneath a haze of sunlight. And her hands. What had previously fascinated me now entranced me. I could make out the veins beneath the muslin-thin skin: pale blue threads as delicate as wiring on a microchip.

I stood, sweating, gasping, shaking, uncaring. My world had shrunk. It now only encompassed me, her and the short space between us. The only sounds were the thudding of my heart, the crinkle of the packages, the bleep of the barcode reader and the roaring in my ears. The only smell was the heady aroma of my euphoria. I clutched the handle of the trolley tightly, afraid I would swoon.

Then she spoke, and I knew in an instant that I had made a mistake.

Dr Hassam gives me drugs. Two white pills, a green pill and a red pill. He says they will make me better.

"I'm okay," I say.

Dr Hassam shakes his head. He holds out the clear plastic cup. If he held his hand over the top and shook it, it would make a sound like maracas.

"Must I?" I say.

Dr Hassam's face remains inscrutable. He should have been Chinese.

"They are for your own benefit," he says. "They will help to redress the chemical imbalance in your brain."

I take the cup and tip the pills into my mouth.

Dr Hassam watches and waits.

"You don't fool me," he says.

He waits some more.

I swallow grimly.

"Good," says Dr Hassam.

She had finished checking out the customer's groceries.

"That'll be sixty-three pounds and seventy-one pence," she said. "Do you have a reward card?"

She did not have Celesta's voice.

I knew how Celesta's voice would sound. Not exactly like the distilled tinkle of mountain springs and the gurgle of a baby and the sigh of a lover all rolled into one. But close, damn close.

Certainly not the scraping, nasal whine that came from her mouth.

"Would you like any cashback?" she whimpered to the customer.

I could not stand it. It offended me to hear that sound issuing from those precious lips. It was an abomination, an obscenity.

That was when I noticed her nametag. It was pinned to the breast-pocket of her striped blue pinafore. The name was embossed in white lettering on a black background. 'Sandra' it read.

Sandra? Sandra?

My reeling senses could take no more. The roaring in my ears intensified, blessedly drowning out her further words to the customer. Tears filled my eyes, blurring my vision, obscuring the nametag. A bitter, coppery taste flooded my mouth. Like blood.

I backed away, the trolley forgotten. I bumped into an obstruction. Another trolley. I backed around it, unaware if its owner spoke to me or not.

Then I was turning, running, fleeing.

I managed to make it outside before doubling up and voiding my stomach onto the rain-slickened surface of the car park.

Celesta, oh, Celesta! I should have worshipped you from afar. Then I would never have known.

The drugs will help me to distinguish the real world from things that aren't really there. So says Dr Hassam.

I pretend that the drugs work, that I can no longer see them.

Dr Hassam is pleased.

"I am pleased," he says. "You are making good progress."

He even smiles. His teeth are nicotine stained.

I smile back. I am pleased that he is pleased.

Then I yawn. The drugs make me sleepy.

This is their only noticeable effect.

They told me how to do it. Whispering, insistent, they first goaded me, taunted me, laughing at me, mocking me.

They will have their fun.

Then their tone changed. They wept when I wept, grew angry when I raged, anguished when I despaired.

And they made suggestions.

They showed me how and where.

I waited in the shadows of the bushes beside the front door.

I crept out of hiding as she inserted the key. Before she could utter a sound, I was in the hall with her, my back against the closed door, hand clamped tightly around her mouth. Around those soft, red lips.

My breath came in short, sharp bursts, but my mind was clear, like my purpose.

They were there, giggling, gloating, telling me the way.

I moved forward, pressing my weight against her, forcing her to move. Half carrying her, I made for the kitchen, careful to maintain my grip on her mouth. If I heard that whine once more, I would go out of my mind. The muffled grunts I could cope with.

I employed my free arm in batting away her arms as they reached for my face or grasped at furniture or door jambs. But I was careful to hit her arms. I didn't want to damage those beautiful, delicate hands.

We made it to the kitchen. They had gone ahead, cavorting in the shadows, directing me with their laughter.

As I reached out to the knife rack and felt her stiffen against me, their giggles grew hysterical.

Dr Hassam does not hate me, I am sure. He might even like me.

He gives me drugs. I swallow them. I sleep.

"Do you still see them?" he asks.

"No," I say.

"Never?" he asks.

"Never," I say.

He nods.

I nod, and sleep.

It did not take long. I had to be careful to avoid her flailing hands. And I had to ensure that I severed the vocal cords. Never again would those soft, red lips be forced to utter whimpering banalities. Whenever they spoke in future, it would be in the lilting tones and profound phrases of my imagination.

As befitting an angel.

Like a good boy scout, I had come prepared. And here's one of life's little ironies: I carried Celesta home in a carrier bag from the very supermarket where she used to work.

How we talked, me and sweet Celesta. I will never forget those precious days we spent together, chatting, gazing into each other's eyes, holding hands.

Until they came for me.

Dr Hassam says that I'm getting better. He says that if I continue to improve at this rate, he may consider transferring me out of the secure unit. And after that, he says, who knows? Of course, he says, I'll have to continue with my medication, even after I've been released.

I nod and smile. Of course, I say. I'll always take my medicine. It stops me seeing things that aren't really there.

Dr Hassam smiles too.

The prosecution pressed for a murder conviction. It was a matter of public policy, it argued. If I was convicted of manslaughter on the grounds of diminished responsibility, it said, there would be a public outcry because of the brutality and mutilation. I had to be restrained.

"Brutality?" I screamed. "Mutilation? I released her! I freed my Celesta. My sweet Celesta."

In the end, the jury didn't find me guilty of murder or manslaughter. In fact, it said I was not guilty of murder.

Due to insanity.

There's always a down side.

I don't always sleep. Sometimes I lie awake, thinking about Celesta. I wonder if she'll be there, waiting for me to get out. If she's not, I'll go looking. I'll find her, sooner or later.

And in the meantime, I'm not alone.

I see them from the corner of my eyes. They know that I'm watching.

They appear, giggling, snide, insinuating. They tell me things.

But they don't fool me.

They're not really there. Dr Hassam says so.

They're not real, are they?

Are they?

The Third Coming

He fled west. Away from the decay, the stench, the silence. Mostly the stench.

He left the city on foot, giving wide berth to the fly-shrouded snarl-ups, avoiding thoroughfares where the congestion was most concentrated.

When he was clear of the knots of stalled cars with their bloated occupants, he approached each vehicle he encountered until he found one that had been abandoned.

Its former owner had not gone far. She lay by the side of the road, staring at the stonewashed sky, wearing an expression of such comic surprise that he started to giggle. Then he noticed the ragged holes in her arms and legs where chunks of flesh had been torn out and he turned away, swallowing hard.

The keys were in the car. After peering and sniffing inside, and tentatively patting the driver's seat, he flung his backpack onto the passenger seat and jumped in.

With only a little coaxing, the engine spluttered to life. The dial showed half a tank of petrol.

He nodded. Enough to reach the hills.

The cottage lay deep in the countryside. He found it by accident after driving through miles of winding narrow lanes and climbing steep dirt tracks that attracted him with their suggestion of remoteness.

The smell emanated from a door in the hallway that gave way under the car jack with a screech of tearing nails. Wooden steps disappeared into deep shadow.

Stench, so thick he could taste it, rose to greet him.

Gagging, he stumbled back into the kitchen. A tea towel hung from a nail next to the cast iron sink. He turned one of the taps. The pipework shuddered, groaned and spat out a stream of thin brown liquid onto the cloth. He tied it around the lower part of his face, lit a paraffin lamp that stood on the kitchen table and returned to the cellar.

Three steps down the creaking staircase, the flickering light revealed the corpses. Two adults, four children, huddled together against a wall. Through the buzzing cloud that enveloped them he glimpsed engorged, pockmarked features. He was about to retreat when he noticed the provisions. Piles of canned food and bottled water stacked around and beneath the stairs.

A dozen sweating, swatting trips later and he had sufficient provisions to withstand a month-long siege.

He wedged the cellar door tightly shut. The cracks he sealed with wet newspaper.

Within a day, the stench had gone.

Most of the daylight hours he spent inside, thick stone walls providing a cool sanctuary from the heat of the July sun that dominated the sky like a proud flaming eye. He read novels and children's books in the light of dancing flames by night, in pools of sunlight spilling in through narrow windows by day. Evenings he spent outside, reclined in a rocking chair, sipping home-made elderflower wine, listening to wood pigeons and watching the sun singe the tops of the mountains that strode away to the north.

Sometimes he wondered about the family shut away in the cellar. As though that would protect them. Maybe it would have if dad or mum hadn't joined the queues of panic buyers to stock up on non-perishables. A breath, a touch from a carrier is all it would have taken. By the time the symptoms showed, the whole family would have been infected.

Other times, when the wine made him maudlin, he thought of his own family. The isolation centre had once been a school, hastily converted when the hospitals and clinics burst at the seams. His mother had gone first, her head cradled in his father's arms. Jamie didn't last much longer, crying out his name in her death throes. His father, so big and strong, slipped away without a whimper. Still they insisted he stayed, amidst the sweat and shit and piss. It was only when the soldiers themselves started to cough, breath rasping, eyes running and haunted behind their masks, that he was able to escape the charnel-house.

He tried to consign these thoughts to the dark vaults of his mind, but they were insistent. As the dying sun's rays were broken down by the prism of his tears, he'd reach for the wine bottle and swig until numb.

Boredom drove him from the cottage. Boredom and a yearning for the taste of fresh meat.

He wandered through the hazy heat of the day across purple moorland, fruitlessly chasing rabbits that flashed their white tails at him, pricking himself on gorse. He climbed a hill, enjoying the breeze that ruffled his hair.

The old man was hidden by the lip of a small depression. He

almost stepped on him.

"Ungh!" The cry was out before he could stop it. He took a step back, fighting the impulse to run.

The man sat cross-legged, faded tee-shirt and shorts revealing thin brown arms and shins. His chin jutted like the jaw of a crescent moon-man, narrow nose curving down to meet it. Wisps of white down clung to the sides of a rounded head that the sun had dyed conker-brown. Eyes the colour of stagnant water peered curiously at him.

"Hello," said the man.

"Who are you?"

The man smiled. "Ah. The impetuosity of youth. But why shouldn't you be direct? These are direct times. You may call me Frank." His grin grew wider. "Yes, that's good. I'll be Frank today."

"I'm Jake."

"You can relax, Jake." Frank spread his hands on his lap. "I am alone. I won't harm you."

"Are you sick? The plague?"

"I am immune. Like you. There will be thousands like us throughout the world."

"The world?" Jake's shoulders sagged. "It's not just here?"

"No. There have been plagues world-wide." His smile faded. "Around ninety-eight per cent of the world's population has perished."

"Ninety-eight. How do you know?"

The old man inclined his head. "Won't you sit? It has been many days since I last saw a living human. I miss conversation."

"Um, I'm hunting. Rabbits."

Frank's smile reappeared as he delved into a rucksack that lay on the ground beside him.

"Like these?" he said, holding two rabbits by their ears.

Jake stared at the limp creatures, his tongue coming out to wet his lips.

He leaned back comfortably against the bank formed by the lip of the hollow and licked fat from his chin.

"That was delicious," he said.

Frank flung a cleanly picked bone into the dying fire, raising a small shower of sparks. "There's nothing quite like the taste of wild coney cooked over an open fire," he said. "Course, I don't need it like you do, but old habits die hard. And I've always enjoyed eating."

"Like you have a choice, right?" Jake laughed. He was more relaxed in the man's presence, confident that Frank had no unhealthy designs upon him. And it felt good simply to be with another person again.

Frank crossed his legs and rested his bony chin upon steepled fingers.

"How old are you, Jake?"

"Nineteen. You?"

"Oh, a good bit older. Want to hear what's been going on?"

"Yes. But how do you know?"

"Let me tell you a story…"

Aeons ago, millennia piled upon millennia, they came.

The creatures sensed their coming like an approaching storm. Some fell with dread and sank to the floor of the swamp. Others fled, instinctively heading for high ground.

Clouds covered the skies in a broiling orange mass. The wind rose, became a hurricane, a hundred hurricanes, tearing up forests, gouging canyons, raising gigantic waves.

The clouds broke apart as it descended. As large as a continent, it landed on the ocean, creating a tidal wave that swept the circumference of the planet and opened fissures in the earth's crust with the might of its passing.

The creatures stood no chance.

"What creatures were these, then?" Jake was not paying close attention. The warmth of the late afternoon sun and his full stomach were conspiring to make him sleepy.

"Oh, many and varied," answered Frank. "Collectively, they are known as dinosaurs."

Jake snorted. "Everybody knows they were wiped out by a meteor. We did that in school."

"That is the accepted wisdom. We have done nothing to correct it."

"Who's 'we'?"

"Permit me to finish the story."

It settled on the ocean's thrashing surface, but did not sink. Not then.

A thousand years passed, more, while storms raged, the earth buckled and spewed, land masses collided and broke apart.

Only when skies had cleared, oceans calmed and tectonic plates locked did they emerge. Only then did they allow their craft to sink.

Some headed west, others east. Once ashore, they began their work.

Jake yawned. "I'm sorry," he said. "I'm not used to spending all day in this heat."

"Do not apologise," said Frank. "I can tell you more in the morning."

"I'd be more interested in learning about the plague."

"I will get to that, I promise. And now, will you stay the night? It is safe."

"Um, not sure." He yawned again. "Not that I have anything to get back for."

When Jake opened his eyes, it had grown dark. Frank sat the other side of the banked fire, face orange in the glow of the embers. His head was tilted backwards, muddy eyes directed to the heavens.

Jake awoke twice more during the night. Each time Frank was gazing intently skywards.

The rich aroma of roasting meat roused him. The sun was already high, promising another scorcher.

"Good morning," said Frank. He sat by the crackling fire, leaning forward to turn the greenstick that held a dripping rabbit carcass.

"Freshly caught?" Jake sat up and rubbed his eyes.

Frank nodded.

"How do you catch them? They scarper soon as I go near them. And, no offence, but I must be quicker on my feet than you."

Frank smiled and placed a finger to his domed forehead. "The mind is fleeter than the foot."

As they ate, Jake watched the old man.

"You were awake all night, weren't you?" said Jake.

"I don't need sleep."

"Everyone needs sleep." He chewed and swallowed with a little grunt. "Do you mind me asking what you're doing out here? I mean, there must be plenty of deserted houses. Why live on a hillside?"

"I'm watching. And waiting."

"For what?"

"They are coming."

"Who are?"

"My people."

"Uh-huh."

A half smile played about the old man's lips. "It's all right to think I'm crazy. Maybe after all this time, I am. A little."

"The plague. Tell me about the plague."

"Smallpox. In Asia, it's Bubonic. Africa, Ebola. That one was a miscalculation. We released it too soon."

Jake stopped chewing. "Released it? What are you talking about?"

"Oh, it's easy. You just walk around brushing against people, pressing push-buttons on pedestrian crossings, grabbing shop door handles, that sort of thing. I did the four cities east of here. Others have done London, Birmingham, Glasgow, and every major population centre in between. The same has happened across the world."

Jake glanced at the half-gnawed leg in his hand. With a grimace, he flung it onto the fire. He stared at the old man.

"Are you seriously saying that you are responsible for the plague?"

Frank returned his stare levelly. "Yes."

The sun was climbing steadily towards its zenith. Jake shivered.

"If you're telling the truth, then you killed my parents and my sister."

Frank shrugged. "They would have died soon. All humans do."

Jake clenched his hands into fists.

"Her name was Jamie." His voice shook. "She was just fifteen."

Slowly, he rose to his feet and took a step towards the old man whose eyes widened.

"Stop," said Frank. "Sit back down. There's no point in hurting me."

"Hurt you? Gonna fucking kill you."

"That won't achieve anything."

"It'll make me feel a lot better."

"No it won't. You ever killed anyone before? Course not. It takes a certain ruthlessness. And it's messy."

Jake took another step towards him. Frank did not move.

"I cannot prevent you killing me," he said, "if that's what you really want. You are young and strong. I am physically frail." He sighed. "There was a time when I could have controlled you. But we lost that power many millennia past."

Jake glared at him, hands clenching and unclenching by his sides. Then his shoulders sagged. He sank to the ground, wrapped his arms around his raised knees and buried his face in them.

"Let me finish what I started to tell you last night." Frank spoke softly. "Then you will understand."

They set the drones to work: hunting, foraging, reproducing. The drones learned quickly. They progressed to herding, clearing, cultivating. They built civilisations. They communicated and traded with, learned from, other civilisations. And warred with them. For violence ran at the core of the drones' being.

Earth's civilisations became great. The drones erected stone circles, monoliths, statues, carved intricate designs in the earth, built temples, ornate tombs, vast cities, fashioned intricate jewellery and curios. Their creations echoed a collective instinct, a genetic memory, an imprint of another place.

The masters were content. All was ready for the Second Coming.

"These drones, they're us. Humans, right?"

"Yes."

"And the masters?"

"My people."

"Right. You're not just some old fart who's been out in the sun too long?"

Frank gazed steadily at him. "I am one of the original settlers. There were five thousand of us. Only half that number remains."

"You're thousands of years old. Uh-huh."

"Many thousands. We constantly regenerate. Any source of energy suffices. Solar rays, for instance." He turned his face to the sun and sighed contentedly. "We did not impart that gift when we created the drones."

"You created us?"

"Yes. In our image, broadly. Your foreheads were more sloping, your bodies hunched. You had more body hair." He laughed. "We thought you might need that protection until you learned how to clothe yourselves. But we equipped you with only the simplest organ to serve as your mind. It has evolved, as have your bodies, to become more like ours. But, it is still a poor copy. Let me see how to explain. It would be like comparing a child's tricycle to a Rolls Royce."

"If you can regenerate, why do you look like that? Why not the body of an athlete and the face of a film star?"

Frank shrugged. "I have always looked this way. It is insignificant. Beauty is measured by the powers of our minds. To my people, I am beautiful, vital, powerful."

"Okay. I'll humour you a bit longer. Why did you create us? For fun? Or were you bored?"

"To fight. We abhor violence. We knew there would be certain obstacles to overcome in order to colonise this planet. As it happened, we did most of your work for you. We had not foreseen our coming would cause extinction of the predominant species. You still had to contend with the mammoth and sabre-toothed tiger, but they were easy pickings compared to a tyrannosaurus."

"This Second Coming you mentioned, what's that?"

The old man winced. "Eleven thousand years ago, the main body of my people came. The craft was smaller than the first—we did not want to repeat the devastation. But something went wrong. We don't know what. The beacon was working—"

"Beacon?"

"Stonehenge to you."

"That's a beacon?"

"Yes." He uttered a short laugh. "It causes us great amusement to listen to you humans postulate theories about it being an ancient calendar or place of pagan sacrifice. My favourite is that it's some sort of stone age computer. But it's merely a beacon, I'm afraid. Simple, but perfectly effective. No, something else went wrong. It descended too quickly, too late to adjust bearings. It crashed on sheet ice in the Arctic. There were no survivors." He shuddered. "The impact partially melted the ice cap. The level of the oceans rose. Many civilisations were destroyed."

"You're a bit careless with your spaceships, Frankie." Jake shook his head. "And to think all that stuff we learned in school about meteors and global warming and ice ages was just so much nonsense."

"Not all. We were only responsible for two periods of devastation.

Others were caused through meteor impact or Earth's own natural cycles. But all that was as nothing compared to the impact on my people. The Second Coming wiped out more than half of our entire population. And we are not a race that reproduces easily. Apart from those of us here on Earth, the only remnant of my species is the few who remained on the planet I once knew as home. They stayed behind to erase traces of our occupation in case those who hunt us should find us." He huddled his arms to his chest. "We did not receive word for many centuries. We feared they had been discovered."

The old man fell silent and stared into the distance. Jake watched his expression sharpen, become a smile.

"Then—what joy!—they contacted us. They had been lying low, were nearly discovered. But the danger had passed and they could make their final preparations to join us. Now they are on their way." He glanced up at the sky, eyes gleaming in the sunlight like burnished oak.

Jake stood.

"Fascinating, I'm sure. But I need a leak."

He turned and moved down the hillside.

Jake jumped at the rustle of his approach, spilling amber drops down his leg.

"Don't be alarmed," said Frank. "I have no desire to harm you. And there is no need to look like that. I have no sexual desires either. At least, not any that you could comprehend. Even less satisfy. I want to demonstrate something."

Frank nodded to their right.

A rabbit nuzzled at a scrubby patch of ground fifteen yards away. Its bright black eyes watched them.

The old man gazed steadily upon the rabbit. He started to walk towards it.

Jake watched him approach the creature, waiting for it to dart away in a white blur. But the rabbit remained still, crouched to the ground, twitching nose its only movement.

Frank reached the rabbit, stooped and picked it up by the scruff of the neck. With one swift motion, he twisted and the rabbit's neck snapped like a dry twig. He walked back to Jake, the lifeless creature dangling from one hand.

"How did you do that?"

Frank tapped his head. "My power lies in here. It still holds sway over lesser creatures. It is only humans who have succeeded in closing their minds to us. But that will soon change when the rest of my people arrive. Together we will be enough to control those of you who have survived."

He walked on to the hollow. Jake stared after him for a moment, then followed.

"Okay," he said. "That trick with Bugs was pretty impressive. But that's all it was. A trick."

The old man looked at Jake, saying nothing.

"Where are you from, Frank? Krypton? Planet X?"

Frank shook his head. "There are no words for where I come from. But I could show you."

"How?"

"You will have to allow me into your mind."

"Yeah. Right."

"It will do you no harm, although the experience might be unpleasant. For us both."

"Are you serious?"

"It is up to you. I cannot enter if you resist. But if you want to know—"

Jake's brow furrowed. "What do I do?"

23

Images flashed through his mind, flickering at first, becoming stronger. Then they ceased to be images. He was there, experiencing them, living them.

A vast, arid landscape, darker than Earth's deserts; dunes shifted in swirling gales, revealing glimpses of subterranean cities, ebony spires and minarets and pyramids and monoliths poking through the sand until submerged by the next gust; great glass domes reflected the red light of the baleful sun that hung low in the sky; movement beneath the domes, scurrying industry, stately processions, meditation and contemplation of an intensity that his senses could never fully comprehend.

Then he was moving away from the surface, passing through the thin atmosphere. He was a ship, blacker than night, vaster than a mountain range, faster than time. An idea glinted at the edge of his consciousness. He grasped at it, snagged it fleetingly. He was riding a wave that pulled him, as a current tugs a leaf, crossing universes in a heartbeat.

Time became meaningless, an abstract concept of little significance, to be thought of—if thought of at all—in the same terms as a young child might consider adulthood.

He looked inwards, seeing row upon row, rank after rank, of drones, stretching to either side and to the horizon. Eyes beneath sloping brows were open, but sightless, thrusting jaws agape in silent screams, tongues slack and lolling in fluid that pulsed to the rhythm of unseen pumps. Coarse pelts rippled like fronds of sea anemones.

His senses expanded, opening to their fullest extent, stretching beyond. A glimpse, nothing more, of inestimable knowledge, of intelligence so greater than his own that he sank, pulped, beneath its weight. In the moment before his overloaded brain burst, he would suffer an instant of such complete insanity that he would not know oblivion when it engulfed him within its infinite grasp.

He screamed.

"Are you all right?" The old man was peering at him closely.

Jake sat in the hollow, near the ashes of the fire, the noon sun lending everything an unreal glare. Leaning to one side, he heaved and vomited half-digested rabbit onto the grass.

"Oh, shit," he groaned, wiping weakly at his mouth.

"Have no fear," said Frank. "I withdrew before any damage was done."

Jake raised his head. "It's all true. Everything you told me."

Frank nodded.

"So we're nothing more than slaves. To your will."

"At first, yes. But you evolved. You closed your minds to us so that we could no longer influence you. At least, most of us could not. There were some who could breach the barrier."

"Yeah? Who, for instance?"

"You have heard of Adolf Hitler?"

"Of course. Are you saying that—?"

"Time can have some effect upon us, you know. Some grew bored, impatient. Some despaired that we were the last. Some went crazy. History, as you call it, is littered with instances. Hitler is one."

"Jesus Christ!"

"Yep. Him too."

Jake blinked. "And the rest of, your people, are on their way?"

"They will arrive soon. Today. But the craft is small. It will create little disturbance."

"I still don't understand. Why the plague?"

"Ah. That was unfortunate. If the Second Coming had succeeded such measures would never have become necessary. You would never have been able to escape our will. But you grew in number, in intelligence. The delay allowed your technology to advance. You became a threat. If my people had arrived before the plague, how would humanity have reacted? By offering the hand of friendship? Or with suspicion and aggression?" He sighed. "It is not mankind's fault. We created you that way."

"Because that served your purpose."

"As I said, we abhor violence."

"You created us to do your dirty work. Then, when it's done, you kill us off like rats."

"Well, that's one way of looking—"

The old man broke off. He cocked his head to one side, his eyes flicking skywards.

Jake raised a hand to shield his eyes and followed his gaze. The sky stretched away to every side, unbroken, bleached nearly white. Unbroken, that is, except to the north. Clouds were gathering above the purple mountaintops. Gathering at an unnatural rate. As Jake watched, more appeared as though the mountains were emitting puffs of shifting smoke.

"At last," breathed Frank. He turned away from Jake and sank to his knees, head tilted back, a rapt expression on his face.

"What will you do, Frank?"

"What?"

"When they've landed. What will you and your people do then?"

The old man turned to look at him. He spread his arms and the joy in his face deepened.

"This is our new home. We will live."

"What about me? And the others who survived the plague? What about humans?"

"I prefer the term 'drone.'" Frank flapped one hand as though warding off a troublesome fly. "We'll put you to work to improve our homeland. First by undoing all the harm your kind has caused."

Jake gritted his teeth.

"What makes you think we'll do what you want?"

A look of impatience was settling into the old man's pointed features and he half turned his head to the sky.

"You will."

Jake glanced up. Clouds were gathering at a frantic pace, like an inkjet from a startled squid. A low booming rumble reached Jake's ears and the centre of the cloud mass parted. What emerged was so huge and so black Jake felt he was looking at absolute nothingness. He sank to his knees with a sigh.

Jake watched the craft's slow descent until the blackness filled the horizon. He turned to the old man who was staring upwards, hands clasped before him as though in prayer.

"I'll find others," hissed Jake, fear lending serpentine sibilance to his speech. "You said there'll be thousands. We'll hide. Resist you. Grow strong again. Then we'll crush you."

Frank turned his head just sufficiently that Jake could read the contempt that curled his top lip into a sneer. "It is too late," he said. "We will not allow you to become strong again. You are drones and will remain drones."

"No!" Jake felt fresh vitality course through his limbs as indignation fuelled rage. He leapt to his feet. "We will fight and overcome you. Starting now!"

Jake bounded over the dead fire, hands held out before him to grab the wattled neck of the old man, fingers already flexing in anticipation of feeling sinew and vertebrae crack beneath them like brandy snap.

Frank's head completed its turn and Jake had time to wonder why the old man's muddy eyes were not filled with fear, but were stirred and alive with something akin to triumph, before his mind was crushed beneath the weight of a thousand immeasurably superior intellects. Grasping, squeezing intellects.

Jake skidded to a halt, less than a foot from where Frank squatted on the ground. He shrieked and clutched at his head. Sinking to his knees, he clawed at his scalp, eyes scrunched tightly shut. Then he stiffened. His arms fell loosely to his sides, chunks of hair and glistening scalp entwined between the fingers. His head dropped forward, chin thudding to chest and teeth snapping shut, severing the tip of his tongue. Jake did not so much as wince.

Frank smiled.

Jake's head slowly came up. His eyes were dull, vacuous, jaw slack. His misshapen tongue lolled from the corner of his mouth dribbling spit and blood down his chin and onto his tee-shirt.

Frank's smile broadened.

"Sit down, drone," he said.

Jake sat.

The Barton Method

I used to get on well with my next-door neighbours. The ones in number 32, I mean. We don't see much of old Mrs Bishop in number 36. Course, she knows where we are should she need us, but she never does. Very independent is Mrs Bishop. Very hard of hearing, too. And very reserved. Unlike our other neighbours.

Edith and I were apprehensive when the Housing Association bought number 32. We had heard the horror stories about neighbours from hell. But we needn't have worried. Cath and Dave were as nice as could be. Down on their luck they might have been, he out of work and she pregnant for the third time when the last thing they needed was another mouth to feed, but they were not resentful or the sort who think that the world owes them a living. And their kids never went without. Lovely kids they were, too, brimming with youthful vigour, but polite and considerate. Respectful, a word that seems largely to have disappeared amongst today's generation.

We were delighted when Dave found a job. Saddened to discover it would mean them leaving the area. Had we known who would be replacing them in number 32, we'd have been mortified.

It had been over a week since Dave and Cath left, with no sign of new occupants next door, when Edith's rose bush was damaged. She loved that rose bush did Edith. It had been my present on our ruby wedding anniversary and produced the most delicate burgundy flowers that gave off a heady scent of summer.

When I stepped into the front garden that morning for a spot of weeding, I noticed two children slouching against the front wall, their backs to me. They looked from their attire as though they were about to go jogging, but I guess that's just current youth fashion.

Talbot Terrace is built on a rise which means that the road and pavement are raised above the level of the front gardens. The top of the wall against which the children were leaning cleared all but our tallest shrubs. I had an unobstructed view of the curved coping stone that was moving under the children's weight.

"Hey! Get away from the wall. It's going to—"

My warning came too late. The stone grated over the bricks beneath it and toppled. The children jumped away, startled, as the stone, a three-foot length of solid concrete, landed on Edith's rose bush. It sheared off three branches, fatally damaging two more, before thudding to the earth under a drift of burgundy petals.

I groaned.

The children peered down at me over the wall. She looked to be about twelve, although I couldn't be sure with all the make-up. The boy must have been a year or two younger. It was he who spoke first.

"It was loose, mister."

I sighed. "I know. It's an old wall."

"Should have it seen to." That was the girl. Something in her voice made me glance up sharply. She was smirking.

"And you shouldn't lean against other people's walls."

"It's a free country, ain't it, Granddad?" Her smirk grew wider. The boy sniggered.

I had been prepared to shrug the matter off. It had clearly been an accident. But as I watched them nudge each other and giggle, my temperature soared.

At that moment a battered transit van pulled up in a cloud of blue smoke. A man and a woman emerged. He was short and stocky, strong-looking. He needed to be to bear the weight of the gold trinkets that adorned him. She was slim, skinny almost, hair dyed scarlet and sticking up like a cockerel's crest.

The man glanced at the children, down at Edith's stricken rose bush, then at me.

"Bit of an accident?" he said.

"The children leaned against the wall and the stone fell." I kept my tone carefully non-accusatory.

The woman stepped up alongside the man.

"Trust us to end up next door to another grumpy old so-and-so," she said, her voice and accent coarse. "C'mon, kids. Before he tries to blame you for anything else."

She shot me a dark glance as she flounced away. The children followed, the girl poking her tongue out, the boy still sniggering. With a sinking heart, I watched the woman open the front door of number 32 with a key.

"Hey, Pops."

I turned back to the man. He was looking at me, eyebrows raised sardonically.

"You want to get this wall seen to." He turned and walked to the van, shaking his head.

That was just the start of it. Over the months that followed our new neighbours burned rubbish in their back garden when Edith had clothes on the line. Our flowers and plants were trampled on, foul graffiti scrawled in chalk on the house walls, refuse scattered over paths. The children graduated from cheek to shouting outright obscenities whenever we encountered them. Our back fence was broken. When Cath and Dave lived there, we had thought about installing a gate between the properties. Now I considered stringing barbed wire over the fence. I caught the boy throwing stones at our cat, Ludwig. The boy ran inside, giggling, as I stood quaking with indignation. Three days later, Ludwig disappeared.

Worst of all was the noise. Every night the thump-thud-thump of music invaded our house. Talbot Terrace dated from the days when houses had been built to last and the wall between us and number 32 was almost a foot thick. Yet they played the music so loudly that the wall might have been made of paper. Night after night, Edith and I lay in bed trying vainly to block out the constant racket. If we thumped on the wall, they turned the music louder. Our nerves grew ragged, our good natures frayed.

I tried reasoning with the woman, only to receive an ear-bashing that made me realise that not all offensive language used by children is learned in the schoolyard. I tried remonstrating with him, only to be met by a steady smirking deflection of any criticism that made my head pound with frustration.

"He makes me want to thump him," I said to Edith after our latest fruitless confrontation.

Edith glanced at me sharply. "William Barton! Don't even think about it. He's the sort who'll goad you into violence and will have you in court before your feet can touch the ground." Her voice softened and she placed a hand on my arm. "Besides, love, he'd make mincemeat of you."

I knew she was right. Even without my bad hips and arthritic fingers, I stood no chance of getting the better of him physically. The knowledge increased my sense of impotence.

"We have to do something," I said. "It's getting so that we're afraid to go outside."

"Let's call the police."

I shook my head. "They'll just say it's domestic. And they'd be right. They've got more important things to deal with."

"What about going to see a solicitor, then?"

"That lot next door will know how to play the system. It'll cost us a fortune. No, we need to do something ourselves."

I thought for a moment, then smiled.

"I've an idea."

I have never liked classical music—Bill Hailey and Elvis are more to my taste—but Edith loves it. Shelf after shelf of vinyl records have been supplemented by row upon row of CDs. Beethoven, Mozart, Tchaikovsky, Brahms, Chopin. Edith listens to them all, the greats and the lesser knowns.

Our CD player was past its prime, the speakers crackly with dust. I went out and purchased a new player, state-of-the-art, with speakers as small as paperbacks that packed an encyclopaedic punch. I also bought one of those hand-held tape recorders like the ones private eyes use on TV to entrap unwitting criminals into giving a taped confession of their sins. They made quite a dent in our meagre savings, but we agreed that if it worked it would be money well spent.

I sat up late night after night, meticulously recording every clash, bang and wallop that emanated from next door, interspersing the action with a taped narrative of the date and times of each burst of noise. Within a few days, I had to buy more tapes, having filled the three that came with the recorder. Each used tape I neatly labelled with the date of recording.

When I had accumulated a month of recordings, we were ready to begin.

Friday night. Edith and I sat in the living room, listening to the steady thump coming from next door. Every now and then, I'd switch on the recorder and tape a few seconds. Eventually the noise died away. I spoke briefly into the tape recorder.

"Two seventeen am, 17th November. The music has just stopped." I switched the recorder off and glanced at Edith.

She reached down to the floor beside her and picked up two pairs of fluffy ear muffs. She tossed one pair to me and we donned them.

Edith nodded.

I turned to our new CD player. When we tested it, it had hurt our eardrums at only half volume. The dial was now turned to two-thirds, speakers facing the dividing wall between us and number 32. The player was loaded with something by Bach, something that sounded harsh and unmelodic to my uncultured ears. I pressed the play button and held my breath.

Despite the ear muffs, the first discordant notes made me jump. I pressed my hands tight to the muffs. Still I could hear the racket crashing from the speakers.

I looked at Edith. She smiled.

Every night leading up to Christmas I'd sit and faithfully record their din. The moment it finished, we'd don our muffs and switch on the CD player. Concertos, symphonies, arias, cantatas, if it was in Edith's collection, we regaled them with it. When they knocked the wall, I'd increase the volume to three-quarters. For an hour we'd let our music play and then we'd go upstairs and collapse onto the bed in blessed silence.

After two weeks of this, a knock came on the door. I answered it.

"Mr Barton?" said the officious looking man who stood there. He flashed a laminated card at me. "Peter Slocombe, Environmental Health Department. I've received a complaint from your next-door neighbours concerning noise pollution coming from your property during antisocial hours."

I held the door wider.

"Come in."

Without waiting to see if he was following me, I strode into the living room. When I glanced round, he was shuffling in behind me, frowning. I took one of the many small cassettes that stood in a neat row on a shelf. I placed it in the recorder and pressed play.

After a few minutes, Mr Slocombe held up a hand and I switched the recorder off.

"Does that happen every night?" he asked. His voice had lost its pompous tone.

I nodded. "Since they moved in during the summer."

He glanced at the CD player.

"For how long have you been—?"

"A fortnight. When they stop, I'll stop."

He looked me in the eye. I held his gaze.

"Mozart? Beethoven?" he said.

I nodded again.

He glanced away, mouth contorting. When he spoke, his voice held a curious hitch.

"Well, I'll be going, Mr Barton. Sorry to have bothered you."

As I watched him walk away, I could have sworn that his shoulders were shaking.

It escalated. They'd play until three in the morning. We'd play until half past four. They played until four. We played until six.

And we didn't confine it to the night. If we found any damage caused to our borders, or rubbish emptied onto our garden, or chalk marks anywhere on our property, we'd give them a blast during the day. Should their children so much as look sideways at us as they played in the garden or street, we'd open the windows and pump Liszt or Elgar at them until they fled indoors.

Nobody else in the street complained. Number 32's occupiers had upset most of them, too. We were inundated with messages of support from all sides. They kept us going through long winter nights, buoyed us as we sat yawning and haggard through Beethoven's Fifth or Handel's Messiah for the twentieth time.

Then came the evening of the last Saturday before Christmas. As usual, I sat poised with tape recorder in hand, waiting for it to begin. When midnight arrived and all we had heard was the howl of the wind and the spatter of rain against the windows, I glanced at Edith. She raised her eyebrows.

Hand in hand, we walked upstairs and went to bed.

The new occupiers of number 32 are not particularly friendly, but they keep themselves to themselves and don't disturb us.

What happened to the previous occupants we have never found out. One morning, not long into the New Year, their van had gone. They had gone. So much for tearful goodbyes, I thought.

The dark circles beneath our eyes have disappeared. We have rediscovered our equanimity. I still don't like Bach, but I can now sit and listen to Mozart or Chopin with no little enjoyment.

And Ludwig came back, purring around Edith's ankles as if he'd never been away.

I read in a newspaper that a chain of supermarkets has started playing classical music outside its stores to discourage unruly youths who hang around making a nuisance of themselves to customers. That made me grin. Maybe I should have taken out a patent on the Barton Method.

The Girl Who Could Fly

"Do you ever dream that you can fly?" The girl watched him intently.

Archer returned her gaze as he considered her question. Around them, the noise and activity in the bar were steadily rising as Saturday night cranked up to fever pitch. Cowboys in dusty denims and battered Stetsons sank beer and eyed women; hustlers prowled around the pool tables, ever ready to hoodwink the unwary; the dance floor began to fill as the four-piece upped the tempo and the cowboys discovered sufficient courage in their bottles to ask the women to dance. Dark sweat stains formed and spread on barmaids' blouses as they upped their own tempo to meet the increasing demand for beer and whiskey. Smoke from countless cigarettes and cheap cigars formed a pall that hung over the room, softening further the muted lighting and preventing the heat generated by the crush of bodies escaping through the panelled ceiling.

Archer was oblivious to his surroundings. He and the girl were sitting far from the dance floor, at a table that had become an island in a broiling sea of revellers. He nodded.

"Yep. I've had dreams where I've flown." He took a sip of his beer. His mind had been feeling pleasantly fuzzy with the effects of the seven or eight beers he'd drunk that evening. It was how he liked to feel on a Saturday night when he was on his own. When Jeanie came with him to the bar, he reined in his drinking, content with her company. Tonight, he had come alone. The fog descending upon his brain had started to lift as soon as the girl sat down opposite him five minutes earlier. Now his head was as clear as the green eyes that stared into his across the stained tabletop. Archer did not mind. At that moment, he would have happily vowed never to drink alcohol again if only he could continue to look into those eyes.

Archer placed his bottle on the table. His gaze never shifting from the girl's, he said, "In those dreams, I don't flap my arms and fly like a bird. I kinda will myself into the air."

The girl nodded as though this was the answer she was expecting. She leaned towards Archer and he felt his breath hitch in his throat as those eyes swam closer.

"Do you enjoy the dreams?"

Archer nodded. He had lost the power of speech far quicker and more effectively than if he'd drunk the bar dry.

Archer fancied that the girl smiled. He could not be sure. He was too immersed in her gaze.

"Come with me," she murmured.

"You did what?" Deputy District Attorney Collins eyed Archer incredulously. "Please repeat that. For the benefit of the jury."

"We flew." As the titters ran round the courtroom, Archer sighed and looked down at his hands. "I know how it sounds."

"Oh, do you? Then perhaps you could confine yourself to the truth."

Archer glanced back up. "I am telling the truth. It's what happened."

"Uh-huh. Just so we're all clear. You left the bar and went up to the roof by the fire escape. But you flew back down."

"Yes." This time the titters were louder.

The Cowpoke and Rustler was only two storeys high, but the ground looked a long way down.

As he had left the sultry atmosphere of the bar, the cold air slammed into Archer like the hoof of a steer, driving the new-found clarity from his mind. He had only the most distant recollection of following the girl up the rickety iron fire escape that clanged and shook beneath his feet. And there had been something odd, something out of place.

Now as he stood on the roof next to the girl and gazed downwards, the ground began to swim in Archer's vision. He raised his head sharply. The sky was punctured with the points of a million stars that gave the night air a ghostly opalescence. Archer barely noticed. The sudden movement had done nothing to correct his equilibrium. Archer swayed.

He put out a foot for balance and stepped into space.

"So did you sprout feathers and soar into the air like a bird?"

"No. I was unsteady… I fell. She grabbed me."

"By the hand?"

"Yes. Her hand was hot. It burned, but like ice, not fire. She fell with me for a moment. Then—"

"Yes?"

"Then we weren't falling. We were, flying. It's the only word to describe it."

"I see. And for how long did you, er, fly?"

"It was prob'ly only seconds. We swooped up into the air and then we floated gently to the ground. It was the most exhilarating thing that's ever happened to me."

"Hmm. Then what happened?"

"I was wiped out, stunned by what had happened. I looked round to thank her, but she'd disappeared."

"In a puff of smoke presumably."

Laughter rang out from the public gallery. Archer's court-appointed attorney rose wearily to his feet. "Objection."

"Withdrawn." Deputy DA Collins waited patiently whilst the judge called for order. His gaze alternated between Archer and the jury, the faintest smile playing around his lips. As the chuckling subsided, he turned the full weight of his regard to Archer. "What did you do then?"

"I went home."

Archer brought the pickup to a dusty halt in front of the ranch house. He yawned as he killed the engine. He opened the door and climbed out of the cabin. Then he stopped dead in his tracks.

"Hello again," said the girl.

"What? How? Did you hide on the back of the truck?" As Archer stared once more into the depths of those green eyes, he discovered that it didn't much matter how she had got there. "But— Jeanie, my wife…" He tailed off as he lost himself once more in that gaze.

"She could fly too. Would she like that?"

Archer recalled the sublime thrill of sliding effortlessly through the air and fresh adrenaline coursed through his veins. He nodded. "I think Jeanie would like that very much."

The girl glanced behind Archer to the water tower that hulked near the ranch hands' quarters.

"I'll fetch her," said Archer. As he made for the house, he broke into a run.

"Your wife was a woman of considerable means, wasn't she, Mr Archer?"

Archer shrugged. "I suppose so. We kept our finances separate."

"Her death has made you a wealthy man, hasn't it?"

"I don't know. I've never cared much for money."

"You cared enough to commit murder."

"No! I didn't—"

"You said earlier that you were unsteady. Were you drunk?"

"No."

"You've heard the testimony of the barmaid at The Cowpoke and Rustler. She said that she'd served you at least seven bottles of beer. Was she lying?"

"No. But—"

"So you weren't sober. Your defence counsellor has called witnesses who have testified to your good character and loving relationship with your wife."

"Yes. What they said was true."

"But drink can change a man, Mr Archer. It can bring out his true inner feelings. You secretly coveted your wife's wealth, didn't you?"

"No! I—"

"You wanted her money and were prepared to kill her to get your hands on it."

"No! No! No!"

"But drink can also make a man careless. It wasn't very clever to push her off the water tower on a bright, starlit night in front of your own employees, was it?"

"I wasn't trying to hurt her. I loved her."

"I have to say, Mr Archer, that you have a strange way of demonstrating it. What most puzzles me, and perhaps you can help me here, is why you didn't kill her out of sight of any witnesses.

Somewhere that her screams wouldn't have been heard by your ranch hands—"

"I wasn't trying to kill her!" Archer had risen half out of his seat. The two armed guards flanking him moved slightly closer.

"So you keep saying. But the evidence does not agree with you. You heard your foreman. He could see you both clearly silhouetted at the top of the tower. He saw you push Jeanie to her death. There was no doubt in his mind as to what happened, or in any of your employees' minds. And they are men who clearly like and admire you."

Archer sagged back into his seat. "Yes, I pushed her."

Archer's attorney was staring at him through grim eyes, his lips compressed into a tight white line; he looked like a man struggling hard not to throw his arms into the air in surrender. Archer ignored him, just as he had when the attorney advised him not to take the witness stand if he was going to persist with his story about the flying girl.

"Might I remind you, Mr Archer," the attorney had said, "that you have been charged with murder in the first degree. In this state, you will face the death penalty if convicted. Have you ever seen a man strapped into the electric chair, Mr Archer? Believe me, it is not a good way to die. Now, if you don't take the stand and we plead insanity—"

"No!" Archer had interjected. "I have to put my side of it, tell the truth. I must make them see that I would never hurt Jeanie. I have to at least try."

The attorney sighed. "It's your funeral."

Now Archer faced the twelve upstanding citizens and looked them in the eye. "Yeah, I pushed her," he repeated, "but only to help her overcome her fear. The girl was holding her hand. They were going to fly… the girl…"

The girl was waiting at the top of the tower. Archer tugged impatiently on Jeanie's hand.

"Will you quit yanking!" said Jeanie. Her giggles had evaporated as they neared the top of the tower and now her voice betrayed her uncertainty. "Look, I've gone along with you so far. Now tell me what's going on, Kelvin. You know how much I hate heights."

Archer looked down at his wife. "It's okay, darling, I promise you. You are about to undergo the most amazing experience of your life."

Archer tugged at Jeanie's hand again, forcing her up the last few steps. As she stumbled onto the wooden platform, Jeanie gasped and came to a sudden stop. Her hazel eyes widened and her mouth gaped open.

The first fingers of unease slipped under the collar of Archer's shirt. "Jeanie? What's the matter?"

She did not reply. She was staring aghast at the girl, her lips moving soundlessly.

Archer uttered a short laugh. "It's okay, darling. This is, oh, I don't know her name. But she's going to show you something wonderful, something out of this world." Archer glanced towards the girl who was standing quietly at the platform's edge. "Aren't you?"

The girl did not reply. She was returning Jeanie's stare, a faint smile touching her lips.

Archer became aware that Jeanie's hand was trembling in his own. She looked away from the girl, but slowly as though it took a lot of will power to force her head to move, and looked into Archer's face. He was shocked to see how wild and staring her eyes had become. Her cheeks were pale and sunken in the milky light.

"Get me away from here, from that thing!"

"Huh? What are you talking about? She won't hurt you. She'll make your dreams come true."

"Oh my God, Kelvin! Have you gone mad? Can't you see what that is? We have to get away! Come on! If we run—"

Jeanie started pulling frantically on Archer's arm. She was babbling, tears pouring down her cheeks.

Alarm bells were ringing madly inside Archer's head, but puzzlement was overriding them. He resisted Jeanie's efforts to pull him back down the stairs and looked at the girl, his brow deeply furrowed.

"Who are you?"

"Who am I? Oh, you already know me. You've always known me. But that doesn't matter now. All that matters is that we can fly, all of us. Fly…"

Archer's brow smoothed as the girl's eyes loomed in his vision until he could see nothing else. The alarm bells' strident tones of warning faded to a distant memory. He was only vaguely aware of Jeanie's increasingly manic efforts to drag him away. He did not release his grip on her hand.

The girl took a step towards them.

That was when Jeanie began to scream.

"Ah. The mystery girl again. Tell me, Mr Archer, how nobody else saw her. You've heard the testimonies. Amy Pierce swears you were alone that night. So do the other witnesses from the bar. Nobody has come forward to say that you were seen talking to anybody. And I'm sure your defence counsellor has tried his damnedest to find someone—anyone—to support your story. Your own ranch hands swear that the only people they saw on the tower were you and Mrs Archer. So—?"

Archer sighed heavily. "I don't know why nobody else saw the girl. All I know is that I saw her. Jeanie too."

"Well, Jeanie's hardly in a position to back you up, is she?"

"Wait! I've just remembered something else. The fire escape. It was old and shaky. It rattled and clanged when I climbed it. But she went up before me. It didn't move or make a noise when she climbed it."

Deputy DA Collins threw up his hands. "Come on, Mr Archer. It's time for the truth, please. We've heard enough about this fictional girl, this girl who could fly." He glanced towards the jury. He had not risen to his position in the DA's office without being able to express utter contempt when the occasion demanded. "So who or what do you suppose this girl was, Mr Archer? Supergirl? Or perhaps an angel?"

Archer sat with his head bowed whilst the judge banged his gavel. As the laughter died down, he looked at Deputy DA Collins through eyes that were distant and haunted. When he spoke, his voice was grave.

"Do you know," he said slowly. "I reckon that's just what she was. An angel, of sorts. Yep. An angel."

The metal cap was lowered slowly onto his shaven head. Brine ran from the sponge, soaked through the black cloth that billowed in time to his ragged breathing and mingled with the salt water that already dampened his cheeks.

Behind the cloth, Archer's eyes opened wide.

"Jeanie," he breathed.

Jeanie smiled. She looked at him steadily from eyes that were now green. She held out her hand.

"Come, my darling," she said. "We can fly. Together. We can fly…"

"Yes," said Archer. "I want to fly."

Room Eight

The girl is pale and waiflike, almost transparent in the pool of light spilling from the hotel porch. She watches me approach, pinched features expressionless.

"All right?" I say.

Her head moves slightly. It might be a nod.

"I'm the new night porter," I say with a smile.

"Oh."

"Er, waitress, are you? Just finished for the night?"

This time I'm certain she nods.

"Right, then," I say. "I'd better get inside. Don't want to be late for my first shift."

I move past her into the porch.

"Watch out for the ghost."

I turn. She's looking at me, eyes shadowed and socketless.

"What ghost?" I step back to her side.

"Of someone who used to work here." Her voice is dull and lifeless. "It only appears at night."

"Have you seen it?"

But she's already walking away, thin shoulders hunched against the night chill, flat black shoes making no sound. Without turning her head, she calls.

"Room eight. Keep away from room eight."

I watch her go, flitting like a moth between the lights that dot each side of the driveway. She is so insubstantial that she seems not to cast a shadow and she disappears from view long before the drive curves round out of sight.

I shiver and go inside.

The manager is dour and uncommunicative. He is fiddling with the alarms when I find him and leaves soon after. It doesn't matter. I've done night portering before and, though I've been out of the business for a few years, I know the job inside out. It's hardly quantum physics.

What a perfect night to start. There are no guests staying and no functions to set up for the following day. I have the luxury of being able to wander the hotel, familiarising myself with the layout.

It doesn't take long. There are only twelve bedrooms, spread along the winding corridors of the upper storey. I poke my head into a couple. They're smartly decorated, perhaps a little flowery for my taste, with functional en suite bathrooms. A tap is dripping in room three, but I can't budge it.

I glance at the door to room eight as I pass. There's nothing out of the ordinary, nothing spooky. Just a wooden door with a brass handle and figure eight at the end of a long corridor. I move on, pretending that what the waitress said hasn't unnerved me. That's easy at first.

"Right on," I say aloud. "I'm in a converted fifteenth-century country house in the middle of nowhere, with only a ghost for company. Just what I want to hear on my first night back." I laugh. The sound hits the walls and dies as though the hotel is absorbing me like a sponge. I don't laugh again.

I soon locate everything I'm likely to need during future shifts. Cleaning materials and vacuum cleaner in an understairs cupboard, crockery in the stainless steel kitchen, cutlery in the restaurant, glasses under the bar. Spare tables and chairs are stored in the garage that forms one arm of an enclosed courtyard. Offices and the laundry room form two more arms, the hotel itself completing the quadrangle.

Behind the offices, beyond the orange glow of sodium lamps affixed to the garage, loom tall black shapes that wave and creak and rustle in the night wind. The trees are hundreds of years old, majestically raising their arms to the sky, indifferent to the affairs of man. A white form takes off and sails above the tree tops, screeching as it goes.

An image pops into my mind. Her. I push it away and go back inside.

The computer behind reception doesn't work. I press the button that should kick-start the screen into flickering animation, but nothing happens.

I ought to clean the public areas, but they look as if they've been done. Carpets are pristine, long expanses of oak at reception and bar gleaming under fresh coats of polish, brass handrails glinting where the security lights catch them. Even the glass panels in the front door have been wiped clean of fingerprints. I press my face up to them and move my head from side to side. Not a smudge or foggy patch remains.

The black backdrop of night makes the glass reflective and I see the deserted foyer behind me, with the oak balustraded staircase sweeping up out of view. For a moment, I know that when I turn there will be someone, or something, standing behind me.

I whirl round, but there's nothing there, not even my own shadow. It's understandable that I'm jumpy. It's been three years, three years to the very night, since I last worked.

My glance strays to the stairs and I begin to climb. Through a set of fire doors and room eight is before me. I walk down the corridor towards it, my footsteps silent on the carpeted floorboards. Pausing only for a heartbeat, I enter.

Room eight is in the gable end of the building and its ceiling is vaulted like the inside of a church. Great oak beams criss-cross at normal ceiling height and above them, in the end wall, is a window through which I can see the pregnant moon behind wisps of scudding clouds.

To my left is a door leading into the bathroom. It stands ajar. Moonlight falls on the edge of a fluffy cream bath towel that awaits the next guest.

I step further into the room. A long dressing table occupies the wall opposite the bed. Beneath it, protruding from the knee space, is a stool, covered in wine velveteen.

Then she is in my mind and I cannot push her away.

Once more I am facing her across the formica-topped kitchen table. She is crying, black hair cascading down face as she stares at her twisting fingers.

"That's it, then?" I'm saying.

"Yes." She looks up. Her eyes are puffy and smudged. "I'm sorry."

Despair worms its way into my heart.

"Please," I say. "I'll be a better husband. We can make a fresh start. I'll forget about him."

She shakes her head and fresh droplets form in the corners of her eyes. I watch them swell like blown glass before they tumble down her cheeks.

"It's over," she whispers. "I'm moving in with him."

"What about Jodie?"

"You can see her whenever you want. You'll always be her father."

Jodie. As her memory slams into me like a slap, I gasp. I'm shaking, beads of sweat covering my brow, and panting like a dog.

I back away, out of room eight.

The Witching Hour approaches. That's what I call four o'clock in the morning. It's the time when everything is still and watchful. Waiting. Even the owls are quiet then.

I suppose it was a mental breakdown. I carried on working for a while, but working alone at night was never going to be good for me in those circumstances. My desolation seemed more complete, more irreversible, at the Witching Hour.

But that was then. Now I'm stronger. The despair hasn't disappeared entirely. I can feel it lurking in the shadows of my soul, ready to surge forward at times of weakness like a black tide. As it just did in room eight. But my defences can cope now, pushing it back patiently and firmly until it is caught again in the shadows, thwarted but ready, ever ready, for the next assault.

There are preventative measures I can take, ways of keeping it at bay.

With the Witching Hour upon me, it is time to busy myself.

I go across to the laundry room, averting my eyes from the swaying menace of the trees. I note the different sizes of tablecloths and napkins, then move into the garage. There I mentally match cloths to tables, napkins to cloths, folds to occasions. Back in the hotel, I study the conference rooms, calculating maximum capacities and working out seating arrangements. I wander around the kitchen, noting the locations of different types of crockery. My gaze plays over the shelves of food stacked in the walk-in fridge. When I lick my lips, it is a reflex. Although I have not eaten, I feel no hunger.

My strategy is successful. By the time I return to reception the first grey threads of daylight are marbling the sky.

I still have hours to wait until I am relieved. With no guests at the hotel, there is no morning staff. But the time passes quickly, without incident.

When the manager arrives, disables the alarms and unlocks the front door I do not approach him. I have nothing to report.

The waitress from the previous night arrives. At some point during the night, somewhere around Witching Hour, I had convinced myself that she was the ghost. She is still pale and insubstantial, but it is approaching midday and she said that the ghost only appears at night. So much for that fine theory, I chuckle to myself.

She doesn't smile, doesn't even look at me, but marches straight past reception and heads for the kitchen. I hear her speaking to the manager. Thinking they might want help setting up the restaurant for lunchtime customers, I follow her.

The manager is standing before a gurgling coffee machine, mug in hand. The girl has donned a white apron and is polishing cutlery with a cloth. Her eyes are wide and she is staring fixedly at the manager as he talks.

Neither of them pays me the slightest bit of attention.

"...porter's night off," the manager is saying. "Hey! Perhaps you saw Alex. It's three years since he, you know..."

As I leave the kitchen, I hear the clatter as the fork she was polishing drops from her hand.

Once more I approach room eight. This time it is illuminated not by moonlight but by thin grey daylight that trickles through the high window. That is not the only difference.

The velveteen-covered stool has moved. It stands in the middle of the space between bed and wall. Above it, tied securely to a sturdy oak beam, hangs a cream bath towel.

She reinvades my thoughts, bringing with her my despair, black and grasping. She is walking away from me, Jodie peering white-faced over her shoulder, calling, "Daddy! Daddy!"

Her last words replay themselves as she glances back.

"Goodbye, Alex."

I bow my head. The stool fills my vision.

As I first did three years ago, I step onto it, my feet making no impression in the cushioned surface. Once more, I reach for the towel…

The Obsessives' Club

The screech of locking tyres and clamour of horn yanked Raymond Poll's attention to more immediate concerns. His eyes opened wide with realisation: the car would not stop in time.

To pause to consider his options was not an option. Poll flung himself forward, feeling his jacket snag on the car's wing mirror. Another blaring horn and squealing tyres, flaring heat in his shoulder, thunder exploding inside his head, then silence.

Poll glanced back. The car had come to a halt beyond the pedestrian island. A white face peered from the driver's window.

Lowering his head, Poll scrambled to his feet. Only raising his eyes enough to avoid onlookers, Poll scuttled away and didn't pause until he'd put a hundred yards between himself and the scene. Ducking down a narrow sidestreet, he stopped.

Poll leant against a grubby building and forced his breathing to slow. Using both hands, he tentatively explored himself, seeking patches of stickiness or swelling. He couldn't even locate areas that were merely sore.

Satisfied that he was unharmed, Poll looked around. The alleyway was flanked by tall buildings that blocked the weak autumnal sunlight. The only sign of life within the shadows was a dirty tabby cat that regarded him stiffly. A steady stream of pedestrians passed along High Street. Poll watched them for a moment. They mostly seemed to be hurrying in the direction from which he'd come, talking animatedly and pointing.

It was only at that moment, as it returned, that Poll realised his hearing had gone. Faintly at first, but growing stronger, like locating a radio frequency, the excited chatter of pedestrians and rumble of engines faded in. Overlying all, another sound: a siren, drawing nearer, its stridency adding urgency to the gait of passing shoppers.

"Police?" muttered Poll. "Did I cause an accident?"

He stepped away from the wall. The tabby's hackles rose and it hissed at Poll like an angry cobra. Poll ignored it. He watched the street, his expression somewhere between yearning and fear. Then, for the first time in his life, he turned and headed away from the action.

The alleyway twisted and wound, growing narrower as its buildings grew darker and taller, becoming more tunnel-like with every step. At any moment, Poll expected it to peter out in the blank rear wall of a drab hotel and he'd be forced to retrace his steps to High Street. He muttered as he walked, cursing his carelessness in drawing such attention to himself. People like Poll craved anonymity, wore it like skin. Within its embrace, they could achieve so much more.

The alleyway at last ended, but not in the obscurity Poll had imagined. There before him, in a black wall that rose higher than he cared to crane his neck to see, stood a door. A yellow door.

He shouldn't have been able to discern any colours in the gloom of that alley. But yellow was most certainly the colour of the door: the yellow of a child's lollipop or a cotton blouse.

Poll glanced back, but could see nothing except more dark walls. He had long left the town centre and blare of sirens behind.

He took a step forward.

The door had no handle, no keyhole, no letterbox, no knocker. Simply a yellow wooden door that fitted snugly into its frame, leaving no gaps that Poll could see.

He sighed, resigned to retracing his route, his mind already working on a strategy to ensure he escaped the police's detection when he emerged once more onto High Street. As he began to turn away, he brought his hand forward, fingers splayed, as though to reassure himself that the door existed.

The wood felt real enough and gave way beneath his touch.

All thoughts of returning to the main road disappeared as the door swung open. Poll stared at the man within the opening.

Short and rotund, the man stood with hands behind back, a posture that accentuated the barrel-like slope of stomach beneath brown waistcoat and jacket. He had a bald head, twinkling eyes and a flowing grey beard that could not conceal the grin that puffed up his cheeks like a hamster's.

Father Christmas in a three-piece suit.

"Mr Poll," said the man. "Do come in. We've been expecting you." His voice was deep and rich, with no trace of accent.

"Expecting me?"

"Why, of course." The man chuckled. "Come along. Come along."

Still chuckling, the man turned and walked further inside. Poll hesitated only a second before stepping past the yellow door.

"Who are you?"

They stood in a blank corridor that, from ceiling to floor, was the same gleaming shade as the door. It brought to Poll's mind something he had not thought about in decades: the congealed lumps of custard he'd been forced to spoon into his mouth and allow to slip down his throat under the baleful glare of the Head Dinner Lady.

The portly man held his stomach as he rocked with merriment.

"My, my, you're an inquisitive fellow," he said. "But I wouldn't have you any other way. I, Mr Poll, am Mr Teufel." He pronounced it, "Toyville". Then he was turning away, beckoning behind with one plump hand. "Come. Come, Mr Poll. Allow me to show you around."

Poll trailed behind as Mr Teufel led him through more corridors that glowed with that pale luminescence as they passed. Sometimes the corridors led straight on like Roman roads; sometimes they wound to the right or to the left, or both at the same time like a two-dimensional corkscrew; at others, they branched into two or three identical-looking passages.

Mr Teufel never dithered, never slowed. He did not glance back or talk, apart from the occasional cheerful, "Come along, Mr Poll," or, "Soon be there," or, "Not far now."

Poll did not ask any more questions. Not that he was still in shock from the incident on High Street; that was long behind him now. He kept his counsel because he was, by nature, a reticent man as befitting someone who did not wish to stand out in a crowd. Poll always dressed incongruously, spoke only when necessary and studiously avoided eye contact.

After what might have been hours or mere minutes—when Poll pondered, he found that it didn't really matter—Mr Teufel drew to a stop. The monotony of rotting primrose walls had at last been broken. He stood in front of a closed door.

The door was half-glazed and wide enough to allow Poll and Mr Teufel to stand side by side before it without touching. Poll, without knowing why, was glad.

The space beyond the door was vast, stretching endlessly away beyond Poll's gaze. Row upon row of plush chairs, like those found in cinemas, filled the floor space. Most were occupied. Poll focused on people sitting nearest the door. Men and women, mainly elderly, slumped in the chairs, staring forward. Many wore intent expressions, brows creased in concentration. Some seemed deeply bored, yawning and slumping so far down in their chairs that it seemed they must soon slip onto the floor. One or two wore expressions of anguish.

Poll pressed his face to the glass and turned his head to see what was occupying their attention. At the front of the hall rose a huge flickering screen. On it, the images of a man and a woman yelled at each other, faces contorted in hate, though no sound reached Poll's ears.

"What is this?" breathed Poll.

Mr Teufel stepped away from the door, grinning broadly. From such close range, Poll noticed that the man's domed forehead and chubby cheeks were florid. Ruddy, maybe, if not for a suggestion of unwholesomeness.

"This is the Soap Room," said Mr Teufel. "Come. The Gamblers are just along here."

Poll followed him to another glass-panelled door. Mr Teufel motioned him forward.

The enormous hall that lay beyond was filled with activity. Thousands of men and women stood in front of flashing fruit machines, feeding coin after coin into slots. Roulette wheels, crap and card tables, countless video screens showing horses thundering over turf, other screens showing greyhounds in manic pursuit of a mechanical rabbit, yet others with boxing matches or football games or basketball flickering endlessly across them. As Poll watched, the light on top of a fruit machine near the door started to revolve and flash amber. The machine spewed a cavalcade of silver coins from its guts. The player slowly bent and scooped up a handful of his winnings. Ponderously, he began to feed the coins back into the machine.

"Why doesn't he quit while he's ahead?" murmured Poll.

"Ah, Mr Poll, to these unfortunates gambling is a compulsion," chuckled Mr Teufel. "To them it's not about winning, it's taking part that counts."

"But some of them look as though they've been in front of those machines for days. Weeks even."

Mr Teufel's grin grew wider as he turned and started down the endless corridor. Poll followed.

As they turned a corner, a man passed them walking in the opposite direction. He shrank away from Mr Teufel, who ignored him, and cast his eyes down as he passed Poll. But not before Poll had time to note the haunted look on the man's face. Poll recognised something about that look, some quality that he had seen before. When he realised where, Poll stopped in his tracks.

"No," he muttered. "I don't look like that, do I?"

Poll swallowed hard and carried on walking.

They paused at more doors. Some of the spaces within were as vast as hollow mountains, some as large as concert halls, others not much bigger than a school gymnasium. Each room contained people engaged in a variety of activities. There was the Alcoholics' Room, the biggest bar that Poll had ever seen, populated by morose, red-veined drinkers; the Gameshow Room where a scowling audience applauded or whooped or oohed and aahed as prompted by a grinning front man; a room bathed in cold green light, filled with men and women who did little except glower at each other.

"What are they doing?" asked Poll.

"Ah, the Green Room," chuckled Mr Teufel. "Every person in there suffers from obsessive jealousy, Mr Poll. They each choose someone and watch them, constantly. If a chosen one should glance in the wrong way or, dare I say, smile at somebody else, sparks fly. If you were to stand there a little longer, you'd see all hell break loose. Ha!" Mr Teufel tittered and put a hand to his mouth like a naughty schoolboy. "But you have plenty of time to study the tragic inhabitants of the Green Room, Mr Poll. Plenty of time indeed. There's so much more to show you yet."

One door was made of ebony and contained only a small paned area, like a letter box, through which Poll peered. The interior was gloomy, starkly furnished with wooden pews. Bowed mourners sat before a priest who cast frequent, though indifferent, glances at a teak coffin standing next to the pulpit.

"There's a chapel here, too?" muttered Poll.

Mr Teufel giggled.

"The Funeral Room," he said. "The mourners are compulsive funeral attenders. Note the relative smallness of the chamber. It's a sad affliction, but rare." From the tone of his voice, Mr Teufel sounded as if he thought it anything but sad.

Poll turned to face Mr Teufel. It was time to put aside his reticence.

"What's going on here? All these rooms filled with compulsive people. All these addicts satisfying their cravings but not getting much enjoyment from them. What is this place?"

Mr Teufel clapped his hands together like an excited child.

"Oh, Mr Poll, found your tongue at last. You may think of this place, my dear man, as a club. A club with very exclusive clientele. A club for obsessives."

"Um. I think, er, yes, I'd like to leave now, please."

"Oh, Mr Poll. You became a member of this club as soon as you stepped across the threshold. I'm delighted to inform you that one of the benefits is permanent residence. And there are no fees. You lucky chap."

"But— you said this is a club for obsessives. I'm not obsessive about anything."

Mr Teufel's grin spread so wide it seemed his chubby face must split like an overripe tomato.

"Not obsessive, Mr Poll? My, but you're a modest chap. What about the hours sitting in darkened rooms watching neighbours through binoculars? The endless vigils outside the windows of strangers, waiting for a glimpse of something forbidden?"

Poll felt heat rise above his neck to envelope his head. He looked down at the yellow floor.

"You see, Mr Poll, you are as obsessive as any other member of this club. Are you married, Mr Poll? No, of course not. Do you have any friends? Certainly not. You have made great sacrifices to feed your obsession. You have forsaken living your own life to watch others live theirs. What greater devotion could a man have, Mr Poll? And if any further proof were needed, what led you here in the first place?"

Poll looked up. Mr Teufel's grin was still in place, but he was watching Poll carefully, red tongue darting out to wet his lips.

"What led me here? I, I—"

"Let me assist, dear sir. You were crossing a busy shopping street and had reached the central pedestrian reservation when you saw them. Is it coming back?"

Poll's brow creased in thought. "The couple. In the window of the flat above the shop. They were kissing. His hand was unbuttoning her blouse…"

"Yes?"

"I stepped back to see properly. I must have stepped onto the road. The car— it nearly hit me. But I managed to avoid it."

"Oh, yes, you avoided the car. Quite a prodigious leap for a man your age. Can you recall why you stepped back into the path of the car?"

"The bus. I saw it from the corner of my eye. It would have blocked my view."

"Indeed, Mr Poll. But the bus kept moving forward. Your great bound took you clean over the central reservation and…?"

Poll gasped. "Into the path of the bus. That was the other horn I heard and the brakes. It was the bus." Poll's knees crumpled and he slumped against the ebony funeral door.

Mr Teufel shook his head.

"You made a considerable mess on the road. An exploding head tends to, you know. The spectacle would have given you the most delectable pleasure had you been able to stay to, ah, rubberneck I think is the modern expression." He nodded sagely. "So you see, Mr Poll, it was your obsession that led you to the Obsessives' Club. My dear chap, you've come home." He began to stroll away.

It took an effort, but Poll managed to rouse himself. He stumbled after his host.

"Wait," he called to Mr Teufel's back.

The man stopped and turned. For the first time, Poll became aware of the odour the other was exuding. A stench of turned milk and spoiled meat that should have made Poll's stomach lurch.

"Which room do I go into?" asked Poll. "Where's the Voyeurs' Room?"

"Oh, there isn't one," chuckled Mr Teufel. "How could there be? How would a voyeur act out his compulsion by skulking inside some room with only others of his ilk? No, Mr Poll, the corridors are your domain."

"What? I don't want to spend any more time in these stinking passages."

"Oh, Mr Poll. It wounds me to hear you speak in such manner about our fine establishment. Just think, my dear man. Unlimited access to the greatest variety of human degradation and misery ever assembled in one place. And no time constraints in which to enjoy viewing them. You might even say you have eternity." His laugh was deep and rolling. "You are indeed most blessed, Mr Poll."

"No. No! I won't spend eternity wandering these wormholes. I won't!"

Poll glanced wildly around. They had stopped near another doorway, one half-paned. He strode up to it and glanced inside. Glassy-eyed people wandered within before an array of screens showing film actors and actresses, popular musicians and sports stars.

"Ah," giggled Mr Teufel. "The Star-Struck Room."

"I like films," said Poll. "I'll stay in here."

His hand went to the door, fumbling for a handle or catch. There wasn't one. He shoved at the door. It didn't budge. He kicked it, rapping on the glass with his knuckles. Nobody inside so much as glanced up. Poll drew back his fist and thumped the glass with all his might. It didn't even rattle in its frame.

Poll's breath hitched in his throat as a sob escaped. He sank to his knees.

"Oh, Mr Poll," said Mr Teufel. "You're a very welcome member of our club. A very welcome member indeed."

Poll raised his head wearily.

"So that's how I get to spend eternity: wandering these corridors with other creeps like me, getting my kicks from spying on other people's misery. Some Heaven this is."

Mr Teufel stood and shook, tears spilling down his red cheeks. The droplets hissed and steamed as they pooled in his moustache.

"Oh, Mr Poll, you're a caution and no mistake. I can see we shall get along famously." He wiped his eyes and gave a great, contented sigh. "Heaven. I must remember that one."

He turned and walked away, his shoulders shaking.

When I Was Young

When I was young, the world was a very different place: neighbourly, less frantic, gentler, yet at the same time harsher and more intolerant.

When I was young, I fought in a war that should have ended all wars, though they said that about the first one too.

When I was young I did something that helped shape the future.

And all I did was duck.

May 1940. I had barely turned nineteen and seen things that today's thirty-year-olds would have difficulty even imagining.

I was part of the British Expeditionary Force sent to the continent to protect France from the threat of Hitler. When Belgium surrendered to Germany, Hitler's blitzkrieg swept into France like a black tidal wave, sweeping all before it.

We fled in tatters. Thousands of us, British and French, made it to the beaches of Dunkirk. There we cowered, grown men reduced to scrabbling like rabbits, waiting to be finished by the advancing German armies or the circling Luftwaffe. We spat out mouthful after mouthful of sand as Stukas completed their sweeps. We scrambled into fresh, flesh-strewn craters, praying that lightning wouldn't strike in the same place twice.

It was not long after the first flotilla of fishing smacks and pleasure yachts appeared defiantly over the horizon, and hope dared to creep into our hearts, that I saw him. Or, rather, heard him.

In the confusion of screaming planes, falling bombs and flying sand, I dived into a shallow crater, only vaguely aware that a beige-clad figure already occupied it. I thrust my face into the sand, hands clasped around my head. As the noise of engines receded and I realised that I had lived through another attack, I became aware of the muttering.

"Gonna kill him. Gonna kill him. Gonna kill him—" It sounded like a mantra in a coarse cockney undertone.

"Go AWOL. Get back to the East End. Who the bleeding 'ell will find me there? Gonna kill him. Gonna kill him—"

I raised my head from the sand. To my left lay a soldier, face down, hands wrapped tightly around his helmetless head. Seemingly unaware of my presence, he continued his monologue.

"Gonna kill him— flippin' great leader, my foot. Gonna kill him. Do the country a favour. Bleedin' Churchill—"

"What?" I couldn't believe my ears. "Oi, you! Shutup!"

His hands dropped away as his head jerked up. He glanced wildly around before noticing me.

"Talkin' to me, mate?"

"Yeah," I said.

Whatever else I was about to say died in my throat, my outrage forgotten. It was his eyes. Large and round and so deep a shade of brown they were almost black. And behind them lay something that unsettled me badly. I had seen madness brought on by extremes of terror and suffering too many times not to recognise it. But the madness that dwelt within his eyes was different. It was deep-rooted, shifting and sly. Malevolent.

His eyes widened as his gaze settled on me, revealing his insanity even more clearly. After all I had been through, all the horror I had witnessed, this was by far the most scared I had ever been.

"You 'eard me," he said.

It was a statement, nothing more, delivered in a flat monotone. Yet it made my fear go up a notch. I instinctively knew that I was in more immediate danger than that presented by all the Stukas Hitler could throw at me.

"Yes," I said. I could see in those shifting black eyes that denial would be pointless. "You were talking about killing Churchill."

His expression did not flicker.

"Gonna do it too," he said. "When I get back to Blighty. Gonna desert, wait my chance then walk up to 'im and shoot 'im between the eyes." As he spoke, he reached inside his tunic and withdrew a revolver. It looked like the type that our officers carried, yet he was a private like me. At the sight of the gun, my stomach tried to swap places with my throat. Now I knew I was in trouble. I also knew something else. He meant to do it. He might not have succeeded, who knows? But I could see in those crazy eyes that he intended to try.

I stole a quick glance to see if there was any help nearby. But the whine of the returning planes was growing steadily louder and every soldier within hailing distance was digging feverishly into the sand. I returned my attention to him.

"Where did you get that?" I said, more to play for time than out of genuine curiosity.

He grinned. In different circumstances it might have made him look handsome. Maybe it was how he had managed to hide his lunacy: by charm.

"Used to belong to that Major Cavill," he said. "Pompous ass!"

"Is he..." I swallowed, trying to find spit. "Is he dead?"

"Must be by now." He raised his voice above the roar of the planes that sounded perilously close. "Leastways 'e ain't going to be in any condition to tell anyone that I've got this." He hefted the revolver in his hand. "You're the only one who knows."

67

"But I don't even know who you are." I shot a glance at my Enfield lying in the sand as he turned the revolver towards me. We both knew that he had time to empty the entire chamber of the revolver before I could so much as grab the rifle, let alone shoot the bolt and level it.

"You could find out," he mouthed. I could no longer hear him.

"No!" My shout was drowned by the diving planes as his finger tightened on the trigger.

In films, bombs always whistle like boiling kettles as they drop. In real life, they sometimes don't. I had developed an extra sense that told me when a silent one was falling nearby. We all had, as otherwise we wouldn't have survived so long, but he must have been too engrossed with shooting me for his to be attuned.

I ducked.

It wouldn't have saved me from the bullet; I was too close to miss. But it saved me from the shrapnel.

The bomb landed behind me, just outside our crater. My duck took me below the lip and protected me from everything except stinging sand. He was kneeling and his chest provided a bed for three jagged chunks of smoking metal. The grin didn't leave his face as he toppled forward, still clutching the revolver.

I never did find out his name. As the bombers wheeled away, I joined the scamper towards the sea. I was picked up by a trawler by the name of Dorset's Pride which delivered me safely to a destroyer that was anchored two hundred yards out. That evening I saw a sight I had never expected to view again: the white cliffs of Dover.

Quite why he intended to assassinate Churchill I will never know. I suspect his reasons were ones that I would not have understood. Not that I agonised about it. When I was young, I didn't always look for reasons. Besides, what reason can be found in war?

And there's something else, something that eighty-odd years on this planet have taught me: sometimes there are no reasons.

Pond Life

Some people believe that a pond is a microcosm of the universe. I've never held to that theory myself. To me, a pond is a pond. Fascinating for all that, but just a pond.

So, what do I know?

Ponds were my speciality. Along with rivers and lakes. I was a biologist, working for the Natural History Museum. Investigation of life and its evolution in our inland waters was what I did. There weren't very many of us. Our distant cousins, the marine biologists, probably outnumbered us twenty to one. But then, they had a lot more water to cover.

We were a strange bunch. We were liable to start off conversations with 'When we all crawled along the sea bed', or, in my case, 'When we all crawled along the pond floor.' You see, I think it just as likely that life originated in our inland waters as flapped out of the ocean.

Biology was my profession, but not my only passion. It was through my other major interest that I learned of the pond.

I'd been a member of the Paranormal Society for ten years or so. I was thirty when these events took place, so that was most of my adult life. Not that I necessarily believed in the paranormal. I'd never seen anything that couldn't be explained by good old science. But I was ready and willing to believe, if there could be no other explanation.

It was in the quarterly newsletter, an amateur production sent out by the local branch of the Society, that I saw it; a short paragraph, four or five lines, tucked away in a corner of an inside page. The headline read: 'Haunted' pond dismissed as natural occurrence. No prizes for guessing which word caught my eye. The paragraph was succinct to the point of banality. I can be even more succinct: an amateur biologist in a West Wales village had attributed a ghostly blue glow emanating from a pond to phosphorescence.

My curiosity was more than a little piqued, and my professional pride more than a little peeved. A ghostly blue glow coming from a pond? Attributed to phosphorescence? And why accept, as the author of the paragraph seemed to have, the word of an amateur biologist? There were people trained and paid to pass such judgements, for goodness sake. Me for one.

I went to see the head of my section, a studious, rotund gentleman named, rather unfortunately I always thought, Malcolm Mudgeworthy. I told him that I had seen a brief mention of a village in West Wales where a pond was emitting a blue glow, said glow being attributed to phosphorescence. I was very careful to omit any reference to ghostliness or the Paranormal Society as Dr Mudgeworthy was the sort of scientist whose world did not allow, could not allow, for anything untoward, anything inexplicable, anything spiritual.

"I'd be quite interested in popping up there to investigate," I said to him.

His goatee twitched as he thought. Just a goatee, mind, no moustache. Looking back, he reminds me of one of those boffins I used to see on television during the seventies expounding earnestly and incomprehensibly on Open University.

"Hmm. A blue glow, you say? From a pond?"

"Yes." I nodded enthusiastically. "Most curious, don't you think?"

"Hmm. Hmm. Maybe some sort of algae, perhaps nourished by a subterranean spring. Hardly worthy of cutting into the budget. Hmm?"

"Well, I have already taken the liberty of checking into accommodation prices in the village." I told him the price of bed and breakfast in the village inn. "I could go for a week and the budget would barely notice." I shrugged. "Couple of tanks of petrol won't break the bank, either. I'll cover any other expenses myself."

Mudgeworthy blinked. "There are places you can stay for that much?"

I knew then that I had him. I pressed home the advantage.

"This local amateur has put the glow down to phosphorescence. I mean, phosphorescence? In Wales?"

"Hmm. Hmm. I agree it's highly improbable. Well, it might be worth looking into. To put the record straight."

I beamed. "Exactly!"

"All right, Mr Watling." I had given up trying to make him call me Graham years ago. "I'll authorise your travelling costs and accommodation expenses for up to one week."

"Excellent! Thank you, Dr Mudgeworthy."

"In which journal did you say you read about this pond?"

"Er, some local rag. I can't remember its name." I waved my hand in a dismissive gesture that I hoped conveyed the insignificance of my source. "Hey! Who knows, I might discover some hitherto unknown microbic life form. We might get papers published, increase our funding. Hell, it could even be named after you. The Mudgeworthy Microbe. How does that sound?"

The goatee twitched again. "Hmm. Hmm. Mudgeworthy Microbe, eh? Hmm."

Traffic was light and by lunchtime I was traversing the South Wales coastal plain. The soft clinking of my specimen jars in the back of the car was soothing and the downpour that erupted as I approached the outskirts of Cardiff did not dampen my spirits. It was only after I passed the old market town of Carmarthen an hour or so later that the constant rain and the swipe, swish, swipe of the windscreen wipers started to grate on my nerves.

And I was lost.

I had to turn off the main road and head away from the coast, towards the foothills of the Cambrian Mountains. The village was situated about ten miles inland, through long, narrow lanes and twisting, bumpy backroads, some little more than tracks. Visibility became increasingly poor as rain mingled with mist to form a grey shroud that cloaked signposts and sapped my spirits. Those signposts that I could read confused me. They were printed in Welsh, although some had the English version immediately below. Not so difficult, you might think. Except that some of the English versions of place names sounded alien and forbidding as I mouthed them aloud to myself. To add to my bewilderment and despondency, I realised that my road map that had led me so unerringly to Carmarthen was now useless. Many of the roads that I needed to traverse were either not shown on the map or else appeared as tiny red squiggles that did not connect to anything in particular. The village was shown on the map, a tiny black dot that could have been a misprint as no roads seemed to connect directly to it.

I drove for more than an hour, my sense of despondency deepening with the gloom outside the car. I was not aware of doubling back or circuiting, yet I saw vague, hummocky shapes of farm buildings that I was sure I had passed before. The metaphysical part of my nature was beginning to override the scientist in me as I started to speculate whether I was searching for a village that did not want to be found, when, cautiously cresting a steep rise, I was there.

The village was a collection of grey stone buildings clustered loosely round a grassed circle (that the locals called 'The Square') in the centre of which rose a majestic, ancient oak that looked as if it had been struck by lightning. The tree's crown had an oddly flattened look as though its uppermost boughs had been sheared off during a cataclysmic storm. Upon closer examination, standing at the trunk and peering up through the leaves, charred remains of broken branches could be seen: black, truncated limbs that twisted tortuously as though they had writhed and turned in on themselves during the inferno.

Half a dozen or so side streets of terraced cottages ran from the Square in straggly tendrils that, I discovered, led nowhere. There was only one road in and out of the village. From the air, the village must have resembled a bloated, spindly spider, black-hearted and greenly venomous with ashen extremities, clinging to a blackened thread.

Of course, the village had a name. Just looking at it written down, all those Ls and Ys and Fs, made my eyes want to spin. I imagined that the only way I could ever come close to pronouncing it correctly was to be ragingly drunk or suffering a heavy chest cold, or both.

The Drover's Arms, my home for the week, was easy to find. The name was attached, in bold letters, to the ubiquitous stone walls of the two-storey building, above multi-paned windows that glowed warmly. A sign protruding from the wall confirmed the name of the establishment below a painted picture of a man in a flat cap herding cattle with a stout stick.

I drove around the tree and parked in front of the inn. Hoisting my holdall and field bag, I stepped out into the steady drizzle.

I have no idea where the man came from. There had been nobody on the pavement as I pulled to the side of the road. As I locked the car and turned towards the building, he was standing in front of me.

Elderly, grizzled cheeks below a flat cap similar to the one in the pub's sign. Water dripped from the brim. He could have been the man upon whom the sign was modelled except that instead of a knobbly drover's stick, he clutched a smooth walking stick.

I stopped, startled.

The man's lips moved and I realised that he had spoken. The words sounded like gibberish.

He spoke again. More gibberish, all spit and undulations, nothing I could get a handle on.

"Sorry?" I said, wanting to move past him and out of the rain, but not wanting to cause offence.

"English, are yew?"

I nodded and smiled, relieved to be able to understand him.

"Not lost are yew, boyo?"

"Er, no," I said. I nodded towards the pub. "I'm staying here."

"We don't get many visitors in these parts, see. Stopping long?"

"Er, few days. Well, I must check in. Um, nice meeting you…"

I took a pace forward, expecting him to step aside. He didn't move.

"What brings yew here then, boyo?" He eyed my bags. "Business, is it?"

I could feel water soaking into my hair and starting to drip down my neck. The warmth emanating from the pub's windows beckoned me.

"Mm," I muttered non-committally. "Must get inside now. Bye."

I stepped to one side and brushed past him, catching a whiff of damp wool and something else, something unpleasant, like the smell of a dank cellar.

As I reached the door of the pub, I glanced back. The old man had turned and was standing watching me. For a moment the drizzle and fading light conspired to make him look different: he had grown taller and much thinner, as though stretched; his eyes had become obsidian

76

and as large as saucers, obscuring his forehead and pushing his cap to the back of his rounded head; his nose and mouth were gone, absorbed into a jaw that had split into two; his dark jacket had torn and lifted, spread out to each side like insectile wings.

I blinked, hard. He became an old man again, standing in the rain, watching me with an expressionless, wizened face.

I turned away and entered The Drover's Arms.

My room was small and basic, but cosy and functional. I slept well that first night, weary from the journey, particularly that last bewildering hour, and lulled by a simple meal and a few pints of the local brew. The Drover's Arms had proved a welcoming place indeed, all dark beams and roaring fireplaces, cheery patrons in the bar and a pleasant landlady. There had been only the slightest communication problem initially. That had soon eased as I grew accustomed to the lilting inflections and the breakneck speed at which the locals spoke.

I awoke to a better day, partial cloud cover allowing frequent glimpses of the strengthening spring sun. The view from my bedroom window was of rolling green meadows and dense black forestry, broken only by hedgerows and a winding cart track. I could see no roads, no other settlements, no farms.

Breakfast was taken at the rear of the ground floor, in a room reserved for eating that I would hesitate to call a restaurant. As with dinner, the food was simple but plentiful. I seemed to be the only guest.

I was served by the landlady, Anna, a widow so I had been informed in hushed tones by a whiskey-swilling, red-faced gent in the bar last night. She was a tall woman, in her early fifties, who moved with an easy, suppressed grace. Her greying hair was bound back tightly giving her face a severe aspect and making her eyes boggle. As I munched bacon and thought about it, I realised that it was not her bound hair that caused her eyes to protrude, it just seemed that way. They bulged naturally from their sockets, green and unblinking, every swivel accentuated by their prominence.

Those eyes were looking at me. Anna stood poised, coffee pot in hand.

"More coffee, Mr Watling?"

"Oh, call me Graham, please."

She smiled. She must have been a striking woman in her younger days.

"Very well, Graham."

"I'd love some more coffee," I said. As she filled my cup, I rustled a scrap of paper from my trousers pocket. "Anna, do you know someone by the name of—" I glanced at the paper, "Gwilym Rees?"

"Old Gwil? Yes. He's a retired schoolteacher. He comes in here every Friday for his G and Ts."

"Do you know where he lives?"

"Oh yes. Everyone knows where Old Gwil lives. It's that sort of village." She laughed, her tongue coming out to wet her lips. "We all know each other's business. Very close-knit, we are."

"Could you direct me to his house?"

"Certainly. Do you know Gwil?"

I shook my head. "I understand he's a bit of an amateur biologist. I have interests in the same field. I'd like to have a chat with him."

She raised her thin eyebrows. The action made her eyes bulge more, almost alarmingly. For a moment I half expected them to pop out onto my plate. "Biologist, is he? There's me thinking he was an English teacher."

I frowned. Biology didn't seem a likely side interest for a teacher of English. "Is there more than one Gwilym Rees in the village?"

"No. There's only one Gwil. One's enough. Here, let me jot down his address. It's not far. Turn left out of here and take the second side street. Gwil lives about a hundred yards on the right." She removed a pen from her apron and scribbled on my scrap of paper. Then she left me to finish my breakfast.

Dressed in my field outfit of canvas trousers, sturdy boots and bottle-green fleece, I enjoyed the short stroll past the giant oak, its leaves shivering in the slight breeze.

Gwil's house was one of a dozen or so identical properties in a stone terrace. The front door, blue and peeling, gave directly onto the pavement. I knocked.

The door was opened by an extremely short man. I'm no giant at a little under six feet, but I towered over him. I looked down onto a liver-spotted head that bore only the vaguest remnant of white, wispy hair. The head inclined upwards and a pair of pale, watery eyes peered blearily at me from beneath heavy lids and a bulbous brow.

I smiled. "Mr Rees?" I enquired. "Gwilym Rees?"

The eyes narrowed. "Yes, that's me. Who are you?"

"My name's Graham Watling. I'm a freshwater biologist with the Natural History Museum." I held out my crumpled card. He barely glanced at it.

"Oh, yes. What do you want?" He spoke slowly in a deep husky tone.

"I'd like to talk to you about the local pond. I saw your name quoted in connection with the, er, phosphorescence. The Museum has sent me to investigate."

He peered at me for a moment. Then he sighed. "I suppose you'd better come in."

He turned and walked away. I followed him, closing the front door behind me. He moved in a rolling motion, his legs bending outwards at the knees as though he rode an invisible horse. But that wasn't the reason for his gait. It had more to do with his girth. He wore grey trousers hitched above the waist by a leather belt. I reckon that three men my size could have fitted inside those trousers, although they would barely reach below our knees.

We went down a narrow passageway and into a gloomy room that smelled of old socks. He motioned to a threadbare armchair which had lost most of its stuffing judging by the way I sank into it. He took a similar chair opposite.

"Where did you see my name mentioned?" he asked.

"You're certainly a man who comes straight to the point," I said, smiling in what I hoped was a disarming way.

"Pah! No point in beating about the bush, is there? So?"

"Fair enough. You were mentioned in a newsletter issued by the Paranormal Society. It mentioned a blue glow seen coming from the pond and that you put it down to phosphorescence."

"Aye. Bloody busybody came poking his nose in, going on about ghosts and whatnot. I told him that to get rid of him. It seemed to have worked too. I didn't count on any scientist types coming here as a result." He looked at me sharply, or at least as sharply as it is possible to look through eyes that seemed to be permanently leaking. "Why is a scientist reading paranormal pap?"

I waved a hand dismissively. "Oh, I'm interested in that sort of thing as a hobby. I take it, then, that you're not an amateur biologist?"

"Nah. Don't know a thing about it." For the first time, he smiled. It didn't suit him. It made him look, well, sort of hungry. "Mind you, neither did the bloke from that society. The phosphorescence thing seemed to satisfy him. Idiot!" He laughed, his hands clasped across his vast belly, his thumbs sticking up. They were extraordinarily long thumbs, thin and finely-tapered, that did not belong on such a podgy man. I also noticed that the skin on the backs of his hands was raised into small lumps and mottled, as though a swarm of ticks had burrowed beneath the surface.

I made myself look up into his face. "Why did you spin him a yarn?

Why not let him investigate and be on his way?"

"Because, Mr er—"

"Watling."

"What if he hadn't come up with a rational explanation for the Dead Lights? He would have published some cock and bull story about other dimensions or something that would have brought crackpots here from all over." He shrugged. "We value our privacy, Mr Watling."

"Mr Rees, you said Dead Lights. What are they?"

"That's what we call the glow that comes from the pond."

"A blue glow? So that bit's true?"

"No point my denying it. Any villager will tell you about it."

"Does it glow all the time?"

He shook his head. "Every few nights. It used to be every night, but it's been reducing now for, well, for quite a while."

"Is there a rational explanation for it?"

He looked at me intently. "You're the scientist, Mr Watling. You tell me."

I nodded slowly. "Where's this pond?"

"I can give you directions, if you're sure you want to see it."

"Why shouldn't I?"

"Are you single?"

"Um, yes. But what's that got to do with—"

"Girlfriend?"

"No." I glanced down at the worn carpet. "We recently split up."

"Any other ties?"

I looked back up, trying to keep my irritation in check. "No."

"All right." He took a deep breath. "There are things in this world that can't be easily explained away, Mr Watling. As a scientist, I expect you do not readily accept that. And yet, you say you are interested in the paranormal. Hmm. A strange combination. But let me warn you that I would be extremely surprised if the Dead Lights could be explained by some theory that your scientific mind would find acceptable. And things that have no rational explanation, well, their effect cannot be predicted. There is no framework within which to do so."

"Yeah, I suppose—"

"What I am saying, Mr Watling, is that you may find more than you anticipate if you pursue your investigation of this, er, phenomenon. You may find answers to questions that you will wish had remained unanswered. You may find things that will bring certain, ah, changes to the way you view this world; indeed, to the way the world views you."

"You seem to know a lot more about this than you've previously indicated, Mr Rees."

"Oh, I'm just a retired English teacher. What could I know? But I do know this much, Mr Watling." He shifted in his seat, bringing his bulk closer. "If you are not prepared to undergo change, and I'm talking about profound alterations to your beliefs, to your life, to the very fabric of your being, then go from this village. Invent a reason for the Dead Lights, something that will satisfy your employers. Forget you ever came here. Otherwise, you may never leave."

I considered for the barest moment.

"Where's this pond?" I said.

It was mating season and I could hear the frogs and toads in full chorus before I could see the pond. It was approached across a well-worn path through a meadow just outside the village, and was set into a natural depression in the land. I glanced back during my approach. I could see the back of The Drover's Arms and realised that my bedroom window overlooked this field. I had not noticed the pond from my window because it was concealed by the grassy hummocks that formed the lip of the depression.

The pond was large as ponds go, perhaps as big as a squash court. The water was a dark healthy brown with patches of green showing where clumps of weeds floated beneath the surface.

I was surprised that no trees grew nearby to provide shade and limit water loss through evaporation in the summer months. I guessed that the pond must be deep and perhaps fed by an underground spring as Dr Mudgeworthy had suggested.

Rushes and water grasses grew abundantly in the shallows at the water's edge, but it was the sheer proliferation of wildlife that took my breath away. I had never seen so many and such a variety of insects and amphibians gathered in such a dense concentration. Water-beetles whirled around the surface or hung just below, collecting oxygen through the protruding tips of their wings, or dived out of sight. Dragonflies, horse flies and damselflies darted and hovered above the water, wings glinting in the sunlight. Pond-skaters and water-boatmen shot across the pond, using surface tension to move as easily as though across ice.

I stood and watched, fascinated. Then I moved forward, having to be careful where I trod as the muddy water edge was littered with every species of frog and toad native to British ponds. This puzzled me: not to see so many species gathered in one place—frogs and, more unusually as they prefer to live on dry land, toads do gather near water in large numbers to mate—but to see them out in daylight. It was my experience that both frogs and toads took no particular delight in the sun, preferring to spend daylight hours in the water or hidden away beneath a stone or log, emerging only in darkness to mate. But these creatures sat on the mud at the water's edge or nestled amongst grass, apparently soaking up the sun. And that wasn't the only thing. They did not all hop away at my approach. Some did, plopping heavily into the water or loping away to find shelter beneath the large stones that dotted the vicinity. But many more stayed where they were, flicking their tongues at passing insects, ignoring me.

I reached the water's edge and crouched, peering into the pond. The body of water was as densely packed with life as the surface and surrounding environs. Frog and toad spawn clustered in jellied masses around the reeds and grass blades; newts swam back and forth, chasing underwater insects and each other; green and brown frogs kicked past, hunting the larvae and nymphs that carpeted the pond floor; a host of other aquatic creatures. I stared, amazed, wondering whether I would be able to purchase more specimen jars locally and would I discover a species as yet unknown to science. With the vast proliferation of species present, this was a distinct and exciting possibility.

My happy thoughts were interrupted by a gradual realisation. The day had grown very still and quiet. I glanced around. All insect activity had stopped. The surface of the water was calm, unruffled by diving beetles or amphibians. And hundreds of pairs of eyes were watching me. Toads, frogs, flies, beetles, even newts below the surface, had stopped what they were doing and had turned to face me, their eyes, green, black, brown and yellow, fixed intently upon me.

I started to rise to my feet, unnerved, when I felt the tremor. I crouched back down and placed one hand on the cool mud. I could feel the vibration rising up as though a piece of heavy machinery had been started up deep below ground. My first panicky thought was that I must be above a coal mine, but then I remembered that I was in farming country.

I felt a thrumming sensation deep within my ears, the sort that occurs when standing close to a pneumatic drill. Yet I could hear no noise. I was surrounded by silence. The hairs on the backs of my hands and neck stood to attention and a sharp smell hit my nostrils, the same odour that I had experienced once before when a house near mine had been struck by lightning: the acrid, charged smell of ozone.

My unease turning to outright alarm, I was rising to my feet when the world returned to normal. The thrumming sensation and smell disappeared. The insects resumed their flitting, the frogs and toads their sunning, the newts their frolicking. The air was filled once again by the sounds of croaking, buzzing and gentle splashing.

I glanced all about to ensure that none of the creatures were still watching me in that curiously human fashion. Then I laughed aloud, feeling foolish, cursing my metaphysical side that had once more gained temporary ascendancy over my mind.

"It is good to laugh," said a voice from behind me.

I whirled around, my nerve endings instantly back on full alert. A young girl stood about ten yards away, watching me. As I peered closely at her, I realised that she was in fact in her early twenties. She walked towards me and I saw why I had mistaken her for someone much younger.

The girl was slight, skinny to the point of gauntness. Her legs protruded from a thigh-length brown skirt, pale and so thin it was a wonder that they could carry her. Legs like Bambi I remember thinking. I could only guess at the shape of her torso as it was concealed beneath a baggy beige cardigan. Her hair was mousy and lank, tied back from her face, emphasising the protrusion of her cheekbones and the sharply pointed nose. Her eyes were small and dark—beady I would call them if I were feeling uncharitable.

The girl stopped by my side, her gaze directed at the pond.

"The Dead Lights will be abroad tonight," she intoned. No sing-song lilt in her voice. It was dull and lifeless.

"How do you know that?" I asked, trying to keep my tone friendly.

The girl continued to stare at the water.

"My name's Graham," I said. "What's yours?"

Just as I thought she would ignore me again, she spoke. "People call me Newt."

"Er, okay. Well, it's nice to meet you, Newt. Do you like coming to the pond?"

The girl looked at me. A spark of animation flared briefly in her eyes. "No! I hate it!"

"Why?"

She sighed. The listlessness returned to her eyes. She looked back at the pond. "I'm so tired," she murmured. "So tired…"

Without looking at me again, she turned and walked back in the direction from which she had come. I watched her go, my heart troubled though I did not know why.

I found that my fascination with the pond had receded, for now at least. I turned and trudged towards the village in the opposite direction that Newt had taken.

It was not far, but I felt inexplicably weary by the time I reached the inn and my head was aching. I climbed the stairs to my room, each step seeming to deplete my energy levels to such an extent that I flopped onto the bed without bothering to undress. I fell into an immediate slumber.

Dream. Something to do with shifting, muted shades of green and a cold, cobalt glow.

Shadows were lengthening across the room as light bled from the sky. I had slept the entire afternoon.

Somebody was knocking at my bedroom door, softly but insistently. I swung my legs off the bed and opened the door. Anna, the landlady, stood there.

She stepped into the room, closing the door behind her. As she walked towards me, she was already hitching up her skirt, revealing lithe white thighs. She was not wearing undergarments.

She pushed me back, unresisting, onto the bed. She straddled me and leaned forward to kiss me. Her breath was hot and moist.

As our lips parted and she began to move her hips, she smiled down at me.

"Hmm," she murmured, "it is the mating season."

I lay in the bath that evening for hours, enjoying the sensation of being immersed in tepid water. I normally preferred to have bathwater as hot as my skin could stand, but not tonight. As I stepped into the steaming water, my skin had crawled in revulsion and pain. I had to hop out and add cold water, lots of cold water.

My throat felt tender and my tongue furry, coarse against my lips, like a cat's tongue.

I became aware that my thumb was rubbing against my forefinger, a circular, almost absent-minded motion. I held up my finger to my eyes. There, nestling at the base of my finger where it met the knuckle, was something that I recognised immediately. It was raised and circular, coarse and grainy. A wart.

With that recognition came something else: a realisation that I had seen this affliction, a far more severe case, already that day. My mind went back twelve hours or so, to when I sat opposite Gwilym Rees and noticed the raised bumps on the backs of his hands. They had been warts too, whole colonies of them.

"What's that?" I muttered. "It's not a what, it's a pimple."

I giggled and let my hand drop back into the cold water.

It was approaching eleven o'clock by the time I left the bathroom and padded down the corridor to my room, a towel wrapped around my waist. A sound like distant thunder erupted from my stomach and I realised that I hadn't eaten since breakfast.

I opened the door to my room and all thoughts of food were driven clean from my mind.

The curtains were open, the overhead light was not switched on, yet I could see clearly. The room was bathed in a cold, blue light.

I ran to the window. The light was coming from the meadow behind the tavern. More precisely, from the pond. The glow washed over the meadow like an ebbing tide, pulsing to some unheard beat.

I dressed frantically and bolted from the room.

A crowd of people three deep lined the edge of the pond, their faces stained in the icy glow, beatific expressions on faces as they gazed intently into the blue water. I glanced quickly around and saw Anna. Near her stood the slight girl known as Newt. I saw Gwilym Rees and, near him, I recognised the old man who had accosted me upon my arrival in the village. He did not lean on his stick but stood erect, swaying slightly in time to the pulse of the light. I recognised other faces I had seen during my short stay. As far as I could tell, the whole village stood staring down into the pond, an air of expectation hanging over them as they waited.

I stared at Anna, tried to catch her eye. She did not look up. No-one paid me the slightest attention.

The thrumming sensation that I had experienced that morning reappeared in my ears. I could feel the vibration emanating upwards through the soles of my boots. As I stood there, uncertain but unafraid, the vibration increased in intensity until it felt as though a pneumatic drill was being operated beneath my feet.

As it seemed the vibration would increase to the point where people would start falling over, it stopped suddenly and completely.

A collective sigh rippled through the assembled villagers and heads turned as one towards Gwilym Rees.

I held my breath.

Old Gwil did not hesitate. He took one step forward so that his foot sunk into water up to his shin. Then he flung his bulk after it in a surprisingly graceful dive that took him towards the centre of the pond. For a moment, his broad back was visible, before he disappeared beneath the surface.

Another sigh went up, louder, a communal expulsion of breath. One by one, villagers followed Old Gwil's lead, stepping into the water and flinging themselves to the centre of the pond before sinking from view. There were no collisions, no two villagers arrived at the centre at the same time. Nobody spoke, but the whole act was carefully orchestrated like an Olympic synchronised swimming team.

I glanced across the pool. Anna looked at me with those boggle eyes that glinted deeply in the blue light. She laughed, the sound carrying sweetly to me across the rippling surface.

"Graham," she called, her voice lilting and ecstatic. "Follow me."

Then she was arcing into the water, graceful as an otter, barely causing a splash.

I paused only to take a deep breath, then dived headlong into the water. Anna looked back and grinned at me. Grinning too, I followed her to the depths.

I saw it all. It was like watching a film in the cinema, with the sound turned to maximum and in smellavision.

A wild storm was lashing the village, rain sweeping down in billowing torrents, thunder reverberating off the low black clouds and sheet lightning depicting the scene in stark white relief.

The village looked different, smaller, cleaner. The only buildings were those clustering around the oak tree—there were no straggling side streets—and the tree itself was shorter, fuller, without the blackened crown. The road that circled the grassed area around the tree was a river of churned mud. A wooden cart rocked from side to side in the gale, its battened wheels leaving the mud in each gust.

The craft emerged from the broiling clouds, a white ball of fire hurtling groundwards at a breathtaking velocity. As it seemed it must smash to the earth, it slowed, a faint pulse of blue flaring briefly at its core. It was no bigger than an overblown beach ball, but its velocity was too great to avert disaster. It landed on the oak tree, causing the topmost branches to burst into flame despite the deluge. Within seconds, they had been obliterated to white ash that the wind whipped away, leaving the boughs below curling in on themselves as they flamed.

The flaming craft bounced upwards, flaring blue again as it struggled to gain height. But it was too badly damaged. It plunged downwards and sidewards, its velocity increasing in the moment before impact.

It struck the surface of the pond, instantly vaporising the water. As the billowing clouds of steam were dispersed by the wind, it sank into the thick mud that formed the floor of the pond. It disappeared quickly, like a heated ball bearing placed onto a slab of butter.

I swam, kicking powerfully with my legs, cutting effortlessly through the blue depths. And I was not alone. There were others swimming all around me, but that is not what I mean. I was not alone in my body: another entity shared my consciousness. We moved our arms and legs together, looked though the same eyes, made decisions together without debate or conscious thought.

I swooped up and down as though flying, turned somersaults, laughed uproariously, my mouth wide open, the inrushing water not affecting me. Anna swam by, grinning, her eyes wide and orange, her thrusting arms glowing green in the Dead Lights.

There was nothing dead about that light. It altered, invigorated, uplifted and, most of all, gave of itself, of its true essence. I opened myself to it, drunk deeply of it, gorged myself upon it.

I looked down, beyond the swimmers below me, trying to peer to the source of the light. It was there, but many fathoms below me, sending the light pulsing upwards in joyous blue waves. I instinctively knew that I could not swim deep enough to see, to truly see. My body, and whatever shared it, could not withstand the tremendous pressure that would exist at such depth. And they could not protect me there, I understood. That was not their purpose.

And what of their purpose? That was simple. It was to give of themselves while they still could.

For they were dying. They had been dying since they had arrived.

I awoke the next morning feeling as energetic and vital as if I was sixteen once more. I whistled on the stairs and sat grinning at the breakfast table waiting for Anna.

She greeted me with a broad grin of her own, her skin glowing youthfully and her bulging eyes glinting greenly.

We chatted like old friends, or comfortable lovers, as she served my breakfast.

I sighed contentedly as I pushed the empty plate away.

"Anna," I said as she came to replenish my coffee cup, "there's something I've been meaning to ask you."

"Ask away," she grinned. "What secrets can we have now?"

"How long has it been since your husband died?"

"Oh, about thirty years. He slipped away in his sleep. Of old age." Her grin broadened. "He couldn't swim."

Dr Mudgeworthy died in 1972, twenty years after the events I have just recounted. That's right. I came to the village in 1952, the year that Queen Elizabeth II ascended to the throne. And she's recently celebrated her Golden Jubilee.

I haven't left the village since.

I've changed over the years. My girth is slightly wider; I have a fair sized colony of warts crusting the backs of my hands. Though neither has reached Old Gwil proportions. Not yet.

My tongue has grown long and narrow, and sticky. I use it to remove lint off clothes. My thumbs have grown, too, thin and tapering. I find them useful for pushing food into my mouth.

And as for my legs… well, they're as strong as tree trunks. Sometimes they feel so packed with raw power that I need to run and jump. So I do.

And swim.

The Dead Lights appear less frequently. They're down to once a week now. No-one knows what will happen when they die. We all sense that the end is near.

Until then, I'll stay here. Help Anna with the pub. We don't get much call upon the bed and breakfast side of things. We like to maintain our privacy here in the village.

The pond is still there, still teeming with life. And we still swim there, once a week.

Sometimes I wonder about them. Is their sole aim survival? If not, will we be able to resist? Will we want to?

Meantime, I try not to worry about the changes that are happening to me, about what I'm turning into.

At the end of the day, the world is just one big pond, right?

The Ruby Slippers

"Some-where o-ver the rainbow…"

The voice floated through the barred opening in the door, down the stark corridor to the small group of men assembled in the Chief Warder's office.

"Is, is that her?" The young priest's voice was low.

The Chief Warder nodded curtly.

"Father—" He glanced down at the papers on his desk. "Father Morgan. Perform Last Rites. Hear her confession. Grant her absolution." He flapped one hand impatiently. "Whatever you people do. But make it quick. She goes at eleven o'clock sharp. Bolger, keep a close eye on the clock."

One of the two men who occupied the cramped space in front of the desk alongside the priest nodded.

"Yes, sir."

The priest glanced at Warder Bolger. The man's eyes gave lie to his appearance of a brutish street-fighter. They were calm and grey and compassionate.

Another line of the song reached the office. Father Morgan repressed a shudder.

"Is she mad?" he asked.

"No," replied the Chief Warder. "Her defence brief tried that one but the shrinks gave him short thrift. Apart from believing she's Judy

Garland in that film, that one from a few years back—"

"The Wizard of Oz, Sir," said Warder Bolger.

"Yes. Apart from believing she's Judy Garland in that film, Clara Blandick is as sane as you or I."

"With respect, she doesn't sound it."

"With respect, Father, that's not your decision. She's been through the judicial process. The King's been petitioned on her behalf. All avenues are now closed to her."

"Oh, yes," came a gleeful voice belonging to the third man who stood before the desk: Warder Lahr. "Today she swings."

The Chief Warder glanced at the wall clock.

"She goes in less than an hour." He stood. "Good luck, Father." He did not offer his handshake.

Warders Bolger and Lahr donned their peaked navy caps and strode from the room. Father Morgan followed. They walked down the corridor towards the singing.

"First time, Father?"

The priest glanced into the dancing eyes of Warder Lahr. He nodded, mouth dry.

Lahr grinned.

"Don't worry, Father. We'll send the mad old bitch on her way. All you have to do is forgive her."

Father Morgan looked away.

"It's not my forgiveness she needs," he muttered.

When they reached the cell door, the singing had been replaced by a low humming.

"Do you know what she did, Father?" asked Warder Bolger.

The priest nodded. "Murdered her elderly neighbour. Loosened mortar in the wall dividing their houses, called her over and shoved the wall on top of her."

"Reckoned she was the Wicked Witch of the West," cackled Lahr.

Bolger's brow crinkled in distaste. He nodded to the priest.

"Ready?"

Father Morgan returned the nod.

Bolger withdrew a large bundle of keys from his pocket, selected one and unlocked the cell door. He disappeared inside.

With a smirk, Lahr followed.

Father Morgan took a deep breath and stepped into the cell.

Bare brick walls and stone-flagged floor were bathed in stark light from a naked bulb set high in the mildewed ceiling. A low brick shelf protruded from one wall; upon it lay a thin mattress and crumpled charcoal blanket. A metal pail emitted an earthy, ammoniated stench. Warders Bolger and Lahr stood either side of the door.

Father Morgan took a pace further into the cell, which brought him to the side of the bed. He looked down at the prisoner.

Clara Blandick sat hunched on the mattress, knees drawn up to chin, rocking gently as she hummed. The shapeless grey shift and tied-back mousy hair made it difficult to guess her age, but Father Morgan knew from perusal of her records that she was forty-six. He also knew that she was single, having sacrificed all hope of a life for herself when leaving home to care for an infirm aunt. The aunt had lived another thirty years and it was only upon her passing that Clara Blandick, as though released from restraint, had begun acting strangely.

It was unfortunate that Clara's next-door neighbour bore a passing resemblance to the actress who, in that Hollywood film about the mythical Land of Oz, played a witch, the arch-enemy of the character portrayed by Judy Garland. Clara had almost been arrested when she hurled a bucket of water over the unfortunate neighbour—"to see if she dissolved," she informed the bemused constable who attended the scene. But the drenched, and kindly, victim had refused to press charges. Six months later, the kindly neighbour was dead, crushed beneath the weight of ten feet of tumbling masonry.

Father Morgan stooped, lowering himself to eye-level with the prisoner.

"Clara," he said softly.

The woman continued to rock and hum, her eyes not so much as flickering in his direction.

"Clara," he repeated, louder.

Still no reaction.

"Dorothy," said Father Morgan.

The humming ceased. The woman turned her head towards him. She had pale green eyes. Child's eyes.

"Who are you?" Her voice was soft and uplilting and innocent. "Have you come to help me return home?"

"I'm Father Morgan. Is there anything I can do for you?"

The woman's bottom lip quivered.

"I've lost Toto," she said. "Are you the wizard?"

Father Morgan ignored the titters coming from Warder Lahr.

"I'm not a wizard, Dorothy," he said. "I'm a priest. Do you understand what's going to happen today?"

Her eyes opened wide.

"You're going to send me back to Kansas?"

Father Morgan breathed in deeply.

"No, Dorothy. You're in prison. Do you remember what you did to the old lady who lived next door? That's why you're here. To be punished. And it's going to happen today. This morning. Soon."

The woman said nothing. She continued to stare at the priest, wide-eyed and uncomprehending.

Father Morgan reached out and placed his hands on top of hers. He could feel that she was grasping something tightly.

"Listen to me, Dorothy. Please! You don't have much time left. I'll hear your confession. We can pray together. Ask the Lord for His forgiveness. Whatever you want."

Her eyes widened further.

"You are the wizard. Please help me go home."

Father Morgan let out his breath in a hiss of frustration. He whirled around to face the warders.

"This isn't right. She doesn't have the faintest idea what's happening to her. This must be stopped."

The smirk on Warder Lahr's face widened. Warder Bolger looked down at the priest, not unkindly, but without any give in his grey eyes.

"It's too late now, Father. What's to be done must be done."

"No! There must be something. Another appeal. A plea for mercy. Something—"

"It's too late, Father."

Father Morgan bowed his head. Slowly he turned back to Clara Blandick. She was fiddling with something about her feet. The priest could now see what she had been clutching so tightly to her chest.

A pair of red shoes glittered in the light from the bare bulb. The woman was pulling them lovingly onto her bare feet. The front of her dress also glinted in the light. Father Morgan looked more closely and could see shiny specks clinging to the coarse material. When he looked again at the shoes, he saw that they were covered liberally in red glitter. Patches of scuffed brown leather showed through where the glitter had fallen away.

"Dorothy?" he said quietly.

She looked up, a smile on her lips. She must once have been a handsome woman, thought Father Morgan. Not pretty, but handsome.

"Do you like my ruby slippers?" she asked. "The good witch Glinda gave them to me."

"You can't wear them," said Warder Lahr. "They're not regulation."

Father Morgan whirled around once more.

"Have a heart, man. What does it matter what shoes she wears?"

Warder Lahr opened his mouth to reply. Warder Bolger beat him to it.

"Shutup, Lahr. She can wear them."

Warder Lahr scowled.

"Suit yourselves." His face brightened. "I suppose it'll be fun watching her kick them off when she does the air foxtrot."

Father Morgan only just managed to stop flinging himself at the man. Hands shaking, he whispered, "You animal."

Lahr sneered.

"Enough!" Warder Bolger stepped forward. "It's time."

The execution chamber was small, walls painted a deep green, the air oppressive. A dozen grim men sat in two rows of chairs arrayed before the gallows. Warder Bolger stood on the wooden platform alongside Clara Blandick. Warder Lahr looked wolfishly on from the floor beside the gantry. Father Morgan stood behind the cramped rows of witnesses, sweating and swallowing, trying to pray for her through his horror.

Clara Blandick had hummed the tune during their walk through the yellow-tiled prison corridors. She hummed it as she climbed the steps to the platform and allowed Warder Bolger to position her so that her red shoes were over the trap door. Only when the warder lowered the black cloth over her face did she stop humming. The cloth bulged in and out raggedly as Warder Bolger fastened the noose securely about her neck.

The only sound to break the heavy silence was the steady ticking of the wall clock. Warder Bolger watched it intently as the second hand strode around to eleven o'clock.

Moments before the hand reached the perpendicular, as Warder Bolger's knuckles whitened on the polished trapdoor release handle, another sound intruded above the ticking.

A click. Then another.

Clara Blandick was tapping the heels of her shoes smartly together.

A third click.

From beneath the cloth bag, came her sweet voice.

"There's no place like home. There's no place like home. There's no place like home—"

The second hand of the clock passed the twelve and Warder Bolger tugged smoothly on the handle. The trapdoor fell away with a loud crash.

There came a collective gasp from the rows of witnesses and a clatter of falling chairs.

Warder Bolger's eyes widened in bewilderment and his jaw drooped.

As the blood drained from Warder Lahr's face, a low moan forced through his lips.

Father Morgan stared at the gallows, a wondering smile beginning to spread across his face.

On the gallows, the slack rope swung as though a stiff breeze had gusted by. The black cloth fluttered empty to the ground.

Mere Survival

(What follows is the translation from Russian of an untitled narrative scrawled on scraps of woodpulp parchment discovered in the early 1950s in a sack outside a village in southern Siberia. The sack also contained strips of flesh subsequently identified to be of human origin.)

I must not sleep. I must not sleep.

Olaf watches me closely from beneath hooded lids. His breathing is light, his expression contemplative. I feel like a tethered goat.

I will write for as long as this pencil stub lasts. My eyelids grow heavy. It takes effort to keep them from sliding shut, to surrender to the netherworld where it is never cold. Even the nightmares would be welcome, such weariness is upon me.

But I must not sleep!

"Did you know," I say to Olaf, "that some people refer to the camps as GULAGs. It's an acronym."

Olaf raises bushy eyebrows that become encrusted with ice as we trek across the tundra through the night, but that now glow tawny in the weak sunshine.

"All I care," he said, "is that I never again enter one."

He yawns and I sit straighter. So does he.

We chose Boris for his bulk. Despite the backbreaking labour, the diet of gruel and maggots, the cramped confinement and the frostbite, he somehow managed to retain a thin covering of flesh over his large-boned frame. Some accused him of thieving or currying special favour with the guards, but nobody ever produced any direct evidence in corroboration. As well for Boris.

I helped punish a fellow prisoner who was caught stealing another's bread. Six of us caught hold of him, dragged him outside and tossed him repeatedly into the air. After the third time he had crashed onto the frozen earth, he had no breath remaining with which to plead. After the eighth time, his ankles, wrists and pelvis were smashed. After the twelfth, his kidneys had become mush.

Some of the watching guards applauded.

The tundra stretches for many hundreds of miles, the bleak monotony only interrupted by the occasional stunted bush. Our boots crunch on lichen and skate over moss as we trudge through the nights. We cannot rest then for the temperature plummets to depths that would mean slow but certain death if we were to lie down on the permafrost with nothing but the thin blankets we carry in our sacks to supplement the woollen rags that clad us. So we move at night, the longest time, forcing our numb feet to keep pacing, afraid to stop, while tears freeze to our eyelids and our beards grow stiff as spun sugar.

Daylight hours are for resting. When the sun has crept above the flat horizon, we wrap ourselves tightly in the blankets and, shivering, fall into fitful slumber.

But not this day. I will only allow my eyes to close today if Olaf sleeps first.

Still he watches me.

Boris needed little persuasion. He was not so dull-witted as to fail to appreciate his danger.

"They talk about you," said Olaf.

"Yes," I said. "They say you are a spy and the guards reward you with extra food."

Boris shook his head.

"I have always been fat," he said. He laughed shortly. "I am now skinny compared to, before."

"They say that you steal food from other prisoners when nobody is watching," I said.

"It is a lie," said Boris.

"No matter," said Olaf. "Once suspicion turns upon you in here..."

He shrugged.

"I will come," said Boris.

"May I borrow your knife?" I say.

A flicker passes over Olaf's eyes and they narrow marginally. But he reaches inside his clothes and tosses over the knife. It is a clasp knife, filched from the workshop, blade whetted to a blue keenness.

I use it to whittle at my pencil stub, being careful not to shave off more than necessary. The stub is too small to allow extravagance.

Closing the blade, I hesitate before lobbing it back to Olaf. He notes the pause, but there is no change in his relaxed demeanour. He knows that he is my physical superior and could retrieve the knife by force if needs must. It would be a mistake on my part to provoke such a confrontation. A fatal mistake.

Olaf grunts as he clutches the knife from the air with one giant fist. He secretes it once more about his person.

I no longer remember the name of the Director of my collective. It was only a mild criticism of him that I uttered, but I was careless after too many vodkas and spoke within hearing of the wrong ears.

They came for me at night, dragging me from bed, silencing Nadia with a rifle butt to the jaw, but thankfully ignoring the screams of my children.

They will have forgotten me by now, just as I have forgotten the Director.

His name burned bright in my mind when I first entered the labour camp, but the desire for vengeance receded in less than a week. Mere survival is a more powerful instinct.

Thousands died in our camp. Thousands died in camps just like it all over the Union. I suspect the aggregate runs into hundreds of thousands. Millions even.

I did not wish to join their ranks. I would not have survived a fourth winter.

Escaping camp was the easy part. The guards kept perfunctory watch at night. Only fools would attempt to cross the frozen wastelands without proper rations and equipment.

It was my suggestion as to how we might create an escape route. All day we refused to surrender to the urge to void our bladders. That night we stood in a close line and aimed at the foot of the fence, where the strands of wire disappeared into the earth. I let go with such a gush that I felt sure the camp would rouse. Such was my relief at releasing the burning pressure on my bladder, for those few blessed moments I did not care that we might be discovered.

When all three of us were empty, we dropped to our knees and scrabbled at the steaming mud. Moving quickly, we scooped out handfuls of muck, tearing fingernails as the earth refroze under our touch.

Olaf rocked back onto his haunches and grunted. Boris stared from me to Olaf, his dark eyes apprehensive.

I grasped at the fence, the blood on my fingertips instantly welding to the metal in an icy seal. The others followed my lead.

"Together," I hissed.

The lowest reaches of the wire were still embedded in the ground, but our day's discomfort had not been in vain. As we took the strain and leaned back, the fence came free with only a faint screech of protest.

I smiled at Olaf.

He shrugged.

Wincing as my fingers tore free of the wire's bitter clutch, I dropped flat to the ground and wriggled through the gap. Olaf followed, grunting as the wire snagged at his threadbare coat. Boris stuck fast.

I hissed down at him.

"Go back and take off your jacket."

He passed the jacket through the gap.

"And your jersey," I added.

He stood shivering in his trousers and ragged vest.

"Hurry," I implored.

As jagged ends of wire gouged runnels in Boris's stomach and chest, I winced and glanced at Olaf. He was regarding Boris much as a cat might watch a mouse. When his tongue darted out to moisten his lips, I looked away.

Boris stood and yanked on his jersey and overcoat.

Shouldering our sacks, we headed into the tundra.

My fingers ache under the strain of clutching what is now barely a nub of wood. Twice my head has lolled against my chest and I have jerked upright to see Olaf sitting forward expectantly. His expression does not flicker as he relaxes his posture once more.

I stand and rub at my legs, trying to force blood through my veins. I clap my hands together and slap at my cheeks.

Olaf snorts.

The stoat disappeared in a flash of ermine before Boris could approach within ten yards. He sank to his knees with an anguished wail.

It wasn't the first creature we had encountered. Cream-coated foxes, snowy rabbits, all had darted away before we could so much as react to their presence.

Boris turned despairing eyes to us.

"What shall we do for food?"

Olaf grunted. I looked away.

Such scraps of bread and weevil-infested oats that we had managed to save for our journey had been consumed by the third day, despite strict rationing. Our cheeks had become sunken, skin sallow beneath cosmetic ruddiness brought on by the raw breezes that swept across the plains.

Water was not a problem. We frequently came across pockets of ice that Olaf chipped away at with his knife, careful not to blunt the cutting edge. Each of us carried containers that we filled with shards and tucked under our armpits as we walked until the ice had melted.

But food, ah, now there's the rub.

I attempted to eat moss, but it stuck in my throat until I was forced to cough it back up. Olaf watched me.

"I had to try," I said.

He shrugged.

"You've tried."

Olaf is complacent. He no longer studies me with the same intensity. His chin has drooped towards his chest once or twice, though I pretend to be too absorbed with my scribbling to notice.

He believes he has me at a disadvantage. He possesses the superior strength. He possesses the knife. He thinks that I must strangle him if he were to succumb to sleep first. He relies on his ability to awake and overcome me before I could accomplish my aim. And he would be right, if strangulation were part of my plan.

I strive to maintain my grips on pencil and consciousness. I count upon his complacency.

That is all I have left.

Boris's eyes snapped open at the touch of steel, but Olaf was too quick. One swift slashing motion and he rocked back on his heels.

I watched Boris jerk and gurgle and clutch at his throat. At the last, I turned away, sure that I would vomit. But instead of erupting, my stomach rumbled.

"Which bits do you want?"

Olaf was regarding me dispassionately, knife held loosely in hand. I swallowed, but could not speak.

Olaf shrugged, turned to Boris and began to slice.

Our calculations were way out. We should have reached some sort of settlement at least two days ago. A town, a village, a farmhouse, anything. But the wilderness extends as far as our weary eyes can see, an unbroken, frozen expanse of nothing.

Our stomachs are once more distended by hunger, cheeks hollow, teeth loose in their gums.

We won't both last another night without sustenance.

The sun dips towards the never-ending horizon.

Olaf's breathing is growing heavier. His mouth expels large plumes, like steam from a toiling locomotive. His glances towards me are becoming fewer. I might outlast him in his complacency. I might.

There is something that Olaf does not know about me. He believes he is the only one who possesses the means to slit another's throat. But I also had access to the camp workshop. My blade is tiny, small enough to conceal in the palm of my hand, but honed to paper-slicing sharpness.

Olaf yawns and his eyes roll momentarily so that the whites show. I do not demonstrate any interest as I have learned from this endless day that any alertness on my part prompts a corresponding awareness in my companion.

So I sit quietly and scribble, blinking my eyelids open as they droop more and more insistently.

In my dreams, Boris is intelligent. He berates me with lashing tongue and smouldering eyes.

"You used me," he says. "I was nothing more than a meal, a walking, talking meal. How valiant of you. How noble. I hope my blood poisons you, that my skin snags on your heart, that my fat clogs your arteries. You will never be rid of me now. I am part of you, a part you will always loathe and fear."

And he reaches for me, fingers clenched into jagged talons, and I try to scream, but my throat is blocked with chunks of raw meat that I cannot shift, and I'm gagging, another man's blood bubbling from my lips and running down my chin...

My pencil has nearly gone. I am struggling to maintain any sort of grip. And there is something else that I have to hold onto. A thought.

I must not sleep.

About the Author

When not inhabiting imaginary worlds that no others can see, Sam Kates—who swears he's sane—lives in South Wales, UK, with a computer and a family. Sometimes he joins them for meals. He has, on occasion, been known to talk to them. To his consternation, they refuse to address him as "Sam."

Author's Note

I know that book reviews on sites like Amazon and Goodreads are considered to be for the benefit of other readers, and rightly so. However, many authors also derive benefit from readers' reviews of their work and I am no exception. So if you are that way inclined, I would be delighted to receive an honest review of this work. Alternatively, if you would like to give feedback but not on a public forum, please feel free to e-mail me at samkates@hotmail.co.uk.

Thank you for purchasing and reading this book.

—Sam Kates
March 2014
samkates.co.uk

Also by this author:

The Cleansing
(Earth Haven: Book One)

The Village of Lost Souls

Lightning Source UK Ltd.
Milton Keynes UK
UKOW06f2119090315
247582UK00018B/637/P